CW00515203

Honore de Balzac

Honorine

outlook

Honore de Balzac

Honorine

1st Edition | ISBN: 978-3-73408-401-0

Place of Publication: Frankfurt am Main, Germany

Year of Publication: 2019

Outlook Verlag GmbH, Germany.

Reproduction of the original.

HONORINE

By Honore De Balzac

Translated by Clara Bell

DEDICATION

To Monsieur Achille Deveria

An affectionate remembrance from the Author.

HONORINE

ADDENDUM

HONORINE

If the French have as great an aversion for traveling as the English have a propensity for it, both English and French have perhaps sufficient reasons. Something better than England is everywhere to be found; whereas it is excessively difficult to find the charms of France outside France. Other countries can show admirable scenery, and they frequently offer greater comfort than that of France, which makes but slow progress in that particular. They sometimes display a bewildering magnificence, grandeur, and luxury; they lack neither grace nor noble manners; but the life of the brain, the talent for conversation, the "Attic salt" so familiar at Paris, the prompt apprehension of what one is thinking, but does not say, the spirit of the unspoken, which is half the French language, is nowhere else to be met with. Hence a Frenchman, whose raillery, as it is, finds so little comprehension, would wither in a foreign land like an uprooted tree. Emigration is counter to the instincts of the French nation. Many Frenchmen, of the kind here in question, have owned to pleasure at seeing the custom-house officers of their native land, which may seem the most daring hyperbole of patriotism.

This preamble is intended to recall to such Frenchmen as have traveled the extreme pleasure they have felt on occasionally finding their native land, like an oasis, in the drawing-room of some diplomate: a pleasure hard to be understood by those who have never left the asphalt of the Boulevard des Italiens, and to whom the Quais of the left bank of the Seine are not really Paris. To find Paris again! Do you know what that means, O Parisians? It is to find—not indeed the cookery of the *Rocher de Cancale* as Borel elaborates it for those who can appreciate it, for that exists only in the Rue Montorgueil—but a meal which reminds you of it! It is to find the wines of France, which out of France are to be regarded as myths, and as rare as the woman of whom I write! It is to find—not the most fashionable pleasantry, for it loses its aroma between Paris and the frontier—but the witty understanding, the critical atmosphere in which the French live, from the poet down to the artisan, from the duchess to the boy in the street.

In 1836, when the Sardinian Court was residing at Genoa, two Parisians, more or less famous, could fancy themselves still in Paris when they found themselves in a palazzo, taken by the French Consul-General, on the hill forming the last fold of the Apennines between the gate of San Tomaso and the well-known lighthouse, which is to be seen in all the keepsake views of Genoa. This palazzo is one of the magnificent villas on which Genoese nobles were wont to spend millions at the time when the aristocratic republic was a power.

If the early night is beautiful anywhere, it surely is at Genoa, after it has rained as it can rain there, in torrents, all the morning; when the clearness of the sea vies with that of the sky; when silence reigns on the quay and in the groves of the villa, and over the marble heads with yawning jaws, from which water mysteriously flows; when the stars are beaming; when the waves of the Mediterranean lap one after another like the avowal of a woman, from whom you drag it word by word. It must be confessed, that the moment when the perfumed air brings fragrance to the lungs and to our day-dreams; when voluptuousness, made visible and ambient as the air, holds you in your easy-chair; when, a spoon in your hand, you sip an ice or a sorbet, the town at your feet and fair woman opposite—such Boccaccio hours can be known only in Italy and on the shores of the Mediterranean.

Imagine to yourself, round the table, the Marquis di Negro, a knight hospitaller to all men of talent on their travels, and the Marquis Damaso Pareto, two Frenchmen disguised as Genoese, a Consul-General with a wife as beautiful as a Madonna, and two silent children—silent because sleep has fallen on them—the French Ambassador and his wife, a secretary to the Embassy who believes himself to be crushed and mischievous; finally, two Parisians, who have come to take leave of the Consul's wife at a splendid dinner, and you will have the picture presented by the terrace of the villa about the middle of May—a picture in which the predominant figure was that of a celebrated woman, on whom all eyes centered now and again, the heroine of this improvised festival.

One of the two Frenchmen was the famous landscape painter, Leon de Lora; the other a well known critic Claude Vignon. They had both come with this lady, one of the glories of the fair sex, Mademoiselle des Touches, known in the literary world by the name of Camille Maupin.

Mademoiselle des Touches had been to Florence on business. With the charming kindness of which she is prodigal, she had brought with her Leon de Lora to show him Italy, and had gone on as far as Rome that he might see the Campagna. She had come by Simplon, and was returning by the Cornice road to Marseilles. She had stopped at Genoa, again on the landscape painter's account. The Consul-General had, of course, wished to do the honors of Genoa, before the arrival of the Court, to a woman whose wealth, name, and position recommend her no less than her talents. Camille Maupin, who knew her Genoa down to its smallest chapels, had left her landscape painter to the care of the diplomate and the two Genoese marquises, and was miserly of her minutes. Though the ambassador was a distinguished man of letters, the celebrated lady had refused to yield to his advances, dreading what the English call an exhibition; but she had drawn in the claws of her refusals when it was proposed that they should spend a farewell day at the Consul's villa. Leon de Lora had told Camille that her presence at the villa was the only return he could make to the Ambassador and his wife, the two Genoese noblemen, the Consul and his wife. So Mademoiselle des Touches had sacrificed one of those days of perfect freedom, which are not always to be had in Paris by those on whom the world has its eye.

Now, the meeting being accounted for, it is easy to understand that etiquette had been banished, as well as a great many women even of the highest rank, who were curious to know whether Camille Maupin's manly talent impaired her grace as a pretty woman, and to see, in a word, whether the trousers showed below her petticoats. After dinner till nine o'clock, when a collation was served, though the conversation had been gay and grave by turns, and constantly enlivened by Leon de Lora's sallies—for he is considered the most roguish wit of Paris to-day—and by the good taste which will surprise no one after the list of guests, literature had scarcely been mentioned. However, the butterfly flittings of this French tilting match were certain to come to it, were it only to flutter over this essentially French subject. But before coming to the turn in the conversation which led the Consul-General to speak, it will not be out of place to give some account of him and his family.

This diplomate, a man of four-and-thirty, who had been married about six years, was the living portrait of Lord Byron. The familiarity of that face makes a description of the Consul's unnecessary. It may, however, be noted that there was no affectation in his dreamy expression. Lord Byron was a poet, and the Consul was poetical; women know and recognize the difference, which explains without justifying some of their attachments. His handsome face, thrown into relief by a delightful nature, had captivated a Genoese heiress. A Genoese heiress! the expression might raise a smile at Genoa, where, in consequence of the inability of daughters to inherit, a woman is rarely rich; but Onorina Pedrotti, the only child of a banker without heirs male, was an exception. Notwithstanding all the flattering advances prompted by a spontaneous passion, the Consul-General had not seemed to wish to marry. Nevertheless, after living in the town for two years, and after certain steps taken by the Ambassador during his visits to the Genoese Court, the marriage was decided on. The young man withdrew his former refusal, less on account of the touching affection of Onorina Pedrotti than by reason of an unknown incident, one of those crises of private life which are so instantly buried under the daily tide of interests that, at a subsequent date, the most natural actions seem inexplicable.

This involution of causes sometimes affects the most serious events of history. This, at any rate, was the opinion of the town of Genoa, where, to some women, the extreme reserve, the melancholy of the French Consul could be explained only by the word passion. It may be remarked, in passing,

4

that women never complain of being the victims of a preference; they are very ready to immolate themselves for the common weal. Onorina Pedrotti, who might have hated the Consul if she had been altogether scorned, loved her *sposo* no less, and perhaps more, when she know that he had loved. Women allow precedence in love affairs. All is well if other women are in question.

A man is not a diplomate with impunity: the *sposo* was as secret as the grave—so secret that the merchants of Genoa chose to regard the young Consul's attitude as premeditated, and the heiress might perhaps have slipped through his fingers if he had not played his part of a love-sick *malade imaginaire*. If it was real, the women thought it too degrading to be believed.

Pedrotti's daughter gave him her love as a consolation; she lulled these unknown griefs in a cradle of tenderness and Italian caresses.

Il Signor Pedrotti had indeed no reason to complain of the choice to which he was driven by his beloved child. Powerful protectors in Paris watched over the young diplomate's fortunes. In accordance with a promise made by the Ambassador to the Consul-General's father-in-law, the young man was created Baron and Commander of the Legion of Honor. Signor Pedrotti himself was made a Count by the King of Sardinia. Onorina's dower was a million of francs. As to the fortune of the Casa Pedrotti, estimated at two millions, made in the corn trade, the young couple came into it within six months of their marriage, for the first and last Count Pedrotti died in January 1831.

Onorina Pedrotti is one of those beautiful Genoese women who, when they are beautiful, are the most magnificent creatures in Italy. Michael Angelo took his models in Genoa for the tomb of Giuliano. Hence the fulness and singular placing of the breast in the figures of Day and Night, which so many critics have thought exaggerated, but which is peculiar to the women of Liguria. A Genoese beauty is no longer to be found excepting under the mezzaro, as at Venice it is met with only under the *fazzioli*. This phenomenon is observed among all fallen nations. The noble type survives only among the populace, as after the burning of a town coins are found hidden in the ashes. And Onorina, an exception as regards her fortune, is no less an exceptional patrician beauty. Recall to mind the figure of Night which Michael Angelo has placed at the feet of the *Pensieroso*, dress her in modern garb, twist that long hair round the magnificent head, a little dark in complexion, set a spark of fire in those dreamy eyes, throw a scarf about the massive bosom, see the long dress, white, embroidered with flowers, imagine the statue sitting upright, with her arms folded like those of Mademoiselle Georges, and you will see before you the Consul's wife, with a boy of six, as handsome as a mother's desire, and a little girl of four on her knees, as beautiful as the type of childhood so laboriously sought out by the sculptor David to grace a tomb.

This beautiful family was the object of Camille's secret study. It struck Mademoiselle des Touches that the Consul looked rather too absent-minded for a perfectly happy man.

Although, throughout the day, the husband and wife had offered her the pleasing spectacle of complete happiness, Camille wondered why one of the most superior men she had ever met, and whom she had seen too in Paris drawing-rooms, remained as Consul-General at Genoa when he possessed a fortune of a hundred odd thousand francs a year. But, at the same time, she had discerned, by many of the little nothings which women perceive with the intelligence of the Arab sage in *Zadig*, that the husband was faithfully devoted. These two handsome creatures would no doubt love each other without a misunderstanding till the end of their days. So Camille said to herself alternately, "What is wrong?—Nothing is wrong," following the misleading symptoms of the Consul's demeanor; and he, it may be said, had the absolute calmness of Englishmen, of savages, of Orientals, and of consummate diplomatists.

In discussing literature, they spoke of the perennial stock-in-trade of the republic of letters—woman's sin. And they presently found themselves confronted by two opinions: When a woman sins, is the man or the woman to blame? The three women present—the Ambassadress, the Consul's wife, and Mademoiselle des Touches, women, of course, of blameless reputations—were without pity for the woman. The men tried to convince these fair flowers of their sex that some virtues might remain in a woman after she had fallen.

"How long are we going to play at hide-and-seek in this way?" said Leon de Lora.

"*Cara vita*, go and put your children to bed, and send me by Gina the little black pocket-book that lies on my Boule cabinet," said the Consul to his wife.

She rose without a reply, which shows that she loved her husband very truly, for she already knew French enough to understand that her husband was getting rid of her.

"I will tell you a story in which I played a part, and after that we can discuss it, for it seems to me childish to practise with the scalpel on an imaginary body. Begin by dissecting a corpse."

Every one prepared to listen, with all the greater readiness because they had all talked enough, and this is the moment to be chosen for telling a story. This, then, is the Consul-General's tale:—

"When I was two-and-twenty, and had taken my degree in law, my old uncle, the Abbe Loraux, then seventy-two years old, felt it necessary to provide me with a protector, and to start me in some career. This excellent man, if not indeed a saint, regarded each year of his life as a fresh gift from God. I need not tell you that the father confessor of a Royal Highness had no difficulty in finding a place for a young man brought up by himself, his sister's only child. So one day, towards the end of the year 1824, this venerable old man, who for five years had been Cure of the White Friars at Paris, came up to the room I had in his house, and said:

"'Get yourself dressed, my dear boy; I am going to introduce you to some one who is willing to engage you as secretary. If I am not mistaken, he may fill my place in the event of God's taking me to Himself. I shall have finished mass at nine o'clock; you have three-quarters of an hour before you. Be ready.'

"'What, uncle! must I say good-bye to this room, where for four years I have been so happy?'

"'I have no fortune to leave you,' said he.

"'Have you not the reputation of your name to leave me, the memory of your good works——?'

"'We need say nothing of that inheritance,' he replied, smiling. 'You do not yet know enough of the world to be aware that a legacy of that kind is hardly likely to be paid, whereas by taking you this morning to M. le Comte'—— Allow me," said the Consul, interrupting himself, "to speak of my protector by his Christian name only, and to call him Comte Octave.—'By taking you this morning to M. le Comte Octave, I hope to secure you his patronage, which, if you are so fortunate as to please that virtuous statesman—as I make no doubt you can—will be worth, at least, as much as the fortune I might have accumulated for you, if my brother-in-law's ruin and my sister's death had not fallen on me like a thunder-bolt from a clear sky.'

"'Are you the Count's director?'

"'If I were, could I place you with him? What priest could be capable of taking advantage of the secrets which he learns at the tribunal of repentance? No; you owe this position to his Highness, the Keeper of the Seals. My dear Maurice, you will be as much at home there as in your father's house. The Count will give you a salary of two thousand four hundred francs, rooms in his house, and an allowance of twelve hundred francs in lieu of feeding you. He will not admit you to his table, nor give you a separate table, for fear of leaving you to the care of servants. I did not accept the offer when it was made to me till I was perfectly certain that Comte Octave's secretary was never to be a mere upper servant. You will have an immense amount of work, for the Count is a great worker; but when you leave him, you will be qualified to fill the highest posts. I need not warn you to be discreet; that is the first virtue of any man who hopes to hold public appointments.'

"You may conceive of my curiosity. Comte Octave, at that time, held one of the highest legal appointments; he was in the confidence of Madame the Dauphiness, who had just got him made a State Minister; he led such a life as the Comte de Serizy, whom you all know, I think; but even more quietly, for his house was in the Marais, Rue Payenne, and he hardly ever entertained. His private life escaped public comment by its hermit-like simplicity and by constant hard work.

"Let me describe my position to you in a few words. Having found in the solemn headmaster of the College Saint-Louis a tutor to whom my uncle delegated his authority, at the age of eighteen I had gone through all the classes; I left school as innocent as a seminarist, full of faith, on quitting Saint-Sulpice. My mother, on her deathbed, had made my uncle promise that I should not become a priest, but I was as pious as though I had to take orders. On leaving college, the Abbe Loraux took me into his house and made me study law. During the four years of study requisite for passing all the examinations, I worked hard, but chiefly at things outside the arid fields of jurisprudence. Weaned from literature as I had been at college, where I lived in the headmaster's house, I had a thirst to quench. As soon as I had read a few modern masterpieces, the works of all the preceding ages were greedily swallowed. I became crazy about the theatre, and for a long time I went every night to the play, though my uncle gave me only a hundred francs a month. This parsimony, to which the good old man was compelled by his regard for the poor, had the effect of keeping a young man's desires within reasonable limits.

"When I went to live with Comte Octave I was not indeed an innocent, but I thought of my rare escapades as crimes. My uncle was so truly angelic, and I was so much afraid of grieving him, that in all those four years I had never spent a night out. The good man would wait till I came in to go to bed. This maternal care had more power to keep me within bounds than the sermons and reproaches with which the life of a young man is diversified in a puritanical home. I was a stranger to the various circles which make up the world of Paris society; I only knew some women of the better sort, and none of the inferior class but those I saw as I walked about, or in the boxes at the play, and then only from the depths of the pit where I sat. If, at that period, any one had said to me, 'You will see Canalis, or Camille Maupin,' I should have felt hot coals in my head and in my bowels. Famous people were to me as gods, who neither spoke, nor walked, nor ate like other mortals.

"How many tales of the Thousand-and-one Nights are comprehended in the ripening of a youth! How many wonderful lamps must we have rubbed before we understand that the True Wonderful Lamp is either luck, or work, or genius. In some men this dream of the aroused spirit is but brief; mine has lasted until now! In those days I always went to sleep as Grand Duke of Tuscany,—as a millionaire,—as beloved by a princess,—or famous! So to enter the service of Comte Octave, and have a hundred louis a year, was entering on independent life. I had glimpses of some chance of getting into society, and seeking for what my heart desired most, a protectress, who would rescue me from the paths of danger, which a young man of two-and-twenty can hardly help treading, however prudent and well brought up he may be. I began to be afraid of myself.

"The persistent study of other people's rights into which I had plunged was not always enough to repress painful imaginings. Yes, sometimes in fancy I threw myself into theatrical life; I thought I could be a great actor; I dreamed of endless triumphs and loves, knowing nothing of the disillusion hidden behind the curtain, as everywhere else—for every stage has its reverse behind the scenes. I have gone out sometimes, my heart boiling, carried away by an impulse to rush hunting through Paris, to attach myself to some handsome woman I might meet, to follow her to her door, watch her, write to her, throw myself on her mercy, and conquer her by sheer force of passion. My poor uncle, a heart consumed by charity, a child of seventy years, as clear-sighted as God, as guileless as a man of genius, no doubt read the tumult of my soul; for when he felt the tether by which he held me strained too tightly and ready to break, he would never fail to say, 'Here, Maurice, you too are poor! Here are twenty francs; go and amuse yourself, you are not a priest!' And if you could have seen the dancing light that gilded his gray eyes, the smile that relaxed his fine lips, puckering the corners of his mouth, the adorable expression of that august face, whose native ugliness was redeemed by the spirit of an apostle, you would understand the feeling which made me answer the Cure of White Friars only with a kiss, as if he had been my mother.

"'In Comte Octave you will find not a master, but a friend,' said my uncle on the way to the Rue Payenne. 'But he is distrustful, or to be more exact, he is cautious. The statesman's friendship can be won only with time; for in spite of his deep insight and his habit of gauging men, he was deceived by the man you are succeeding, and nearly became a victim to his abuse of confidence. This is enough to guide you in your behavior to him.'

"When we knocked at the enormous outer door of a house as large as the Hotel Carnavalet, with a courtyard in front and a garden behind, the sound rang as in a desert. While my uncle inquired of an old porter in livery if the

Count were at home, I cast my eyes, seeing everything at once, over the courtyard where the cobblestones were hidden in the grass, the blackened walls where little gardens were flourishing above the decorations of the elegant architecture, and on the roof, as high as that of the Tuileries. The balustrade of the upper balconies was eaten away. Through a magnificent colonnade I could see a second court on one side, where were the offices; the door was rotting. An old coachman was there cleaning an old carriage. The indifferent air of this servant allowed me to assume that the handsome stables, where of old so many horses had whinnied, now sheltered two at most. The handsome facade of the house seemed to me gloomy, like that of a mansion belonging to the State or the Crown, and given up to some public office. A bell rang as we walked across, my uncle and I, from the porter's lodge —*Inquire of the Porter* was still written over the door—towards the outside steps, where a footman came out in a livery like that of Labranche at the Theatre Francais in the old stock plays. A visitor was so rare that the servant was putting his coat on when he opened a glass door with small panes, on each side of which the smoke of a lamp had traced patterns on the walls.

"A hall so magnificent as to be worthy of Versailles ended in a staircase such as will never again be built in France, taking up as much space as the whole of a modern house. As we went up the marble steps, as cold as tombstones, and wide enough for eight persons to walk abreast, our tread echoed under sonorous vaulting. The banister charmed the eye by its miraculous workmanship—goldsmith's work in iron—wrought by the fancy of an artist of the time of Henri III. Chilled as by an icy mantle that fell on our shoulders, we went through ante-rooms, drawing-rooms opening one out of the other, with carpetless parquet floors, and furnished with such splendid antiquities as from thence would find their way to the curiosity dealers. At last we reached a large study in a cross wing, with all the windows looking into an immense garden.

"'Monsieur le Cure of the White Friars, and his nephew, Monsieur de l'Hostal,' said Labranche, to whose care the other theatrical servant had consigned us in the first ante-chamber.

"Comte Octave, dressed in long trousers and a gray flannel morning coat, rose from his seat by a huge writing-table, came to the fireplace, and signed to me to sit down, while he went forward to take my uncle's hands, which he pressed.

"'Though I am in the parish of Saint-Paul,' said he, 'I could scarcely have failed to hear of the Cure of the White Friars, and I am happy to make his acquaintance.'

"'Your Excellency is most kind,' replied my uncle. 'I have brought to you my only remaining relation. While I believe that I am offering a good gift to your Excellency, I hope at the same time to give my nephew a second father.'

"'As to that, I can only reply, Monsieur l'Abbe, when we shall have tried each other,' said Comte Octave. 'Your name?' he added to me.

"'Maurice.'

"'He has taken his doctor's degree in law,' my uncle observed.

"'Very good, very good!' said the Count, looking at me from head to foot. 'Monsieur l'Abbe, I hope that for your nephew's sake in the first instance, and then for mine, you will do me the honor of dining here every Monday. That will be our family dinner, our family party.'

"My uncle and the Count then began to talk of religion from the political point of view, of charitable institutes, the repression of crime, and I could at my leisure study the man on whom my fate would henceforth depend. The Count was of middle height; it was impossible to judge of his build on account of his dress, but he seemed to me to be lean and spare. His face was harsh and hollow; the features were refined. His mouth, which was rather large, expressed both irony and kindliness. His forehead perhaps too spacious, was as intimidating as that of a madman, all the more so from the contrast of the lower part of the face, which ended squarely in a short chin very near the lower lip. Small eyes, of turquoise blue, were as keen and bright as those of the Prince de Talleyrand—which I admired at a later time—and endowed, like the Prince's, with the faculty of becoming expressionless to the verge of gloom; and they added to the singularity of a face that was not pale but yellow. This complexion seemed to bespeak an irritable temper and violent passions. His hair, already silvered, and carefully dressed, seemed to furrow his head with streaks of black and white alternately. The trimness of this head spoiled the resemblance I had remarked in the Count to the wonderful monk described by Lewis after Schedoni in the *Confessional of the Black Penitents (The Italian)*, a superior creation, as it seems to me, to *The Monk*.

"The Count was already shaved, having to attend early at the law courts. Two candelabra with four lights, screened by lamp-shades, were still burning at the opposite ends of the writing-table, and showed plainly that the magistrate rose long before daylight. His hands, which I saw when he took hold of the bell-pull to summon his servant, were extremely fine, and as white as a woman's.

"As I tell you this story," said the Consul-General, interrupting himself, "I am altering the titles and the social position of this gentleman, while placing him in circumstances analogous to what his really were. His profession, rank, luxury, fortune, and style of living were the same; all these details are true, but I would not be false to my benefactor, nor to my usual habits of discretion.

"Instead of feeling—as I really was, socially speaking—an insect in the presence of an eagle," the narrator went on after a pause, "I felt I know not what indefinable impression from the Count's appearance, which, however, I can now account for. Artists of genius" (and he bowed gracefully to the Ambassador, the distinguished lady, and the two Frenchmen), "real statesmen, poets, a general who has commanded armies—in short, all really great minds are simple, and their simplicity places you on a level with themselves.—You who are all of superior minds," he said, addressing his guests, "have perhaps observed how feeling can bridge over the distances created by society. If we are inferior to you in intellect, we can be your equals in devoted friendship. By the temperature—allow me the word—of our hearts I felt myself as near my patron as I was far below him in rank. In short, the soul has its clairvoyance; it has presentiments of suffering, grief, joy, antagonism, or hatred in others.

"I vaguely discerned the symptoms of a mystery, from recognizing in the Count the same effects of physiognomy as I had observed in my uncle. The exercise of virtue, serenity of conscience, and purity of mind had transfigured my uncle, who from being ugly had become quite beautiful. I detected a metamorphosis of a reverse kind in the Count's face; at the first glance I thought he was about fifty-five, but after an attentive examination I found youth entombed under the ice of a great sorrow, under the fatigue of persistent study, under the glowing hues of some suppressed passion. At a word from my uncle the Count's eyes recovered for a moment the softness of the periwinkle flower, and he had an admiring smile, which revealed what I believed to be his real age, about forty. These observations I made, not then but afterwards, as I recalled the circumstances of my visit.

"The man-servant came in carrying a tray with his master's breakfast on it.

"'I did not ask for breakfast,' remarked the Count; 'but leave it, and show monsieur to his rooms.'

"I followed the servant, who led the way to a complete set of pretty rooms, under a terrace, between the great courtyard and the servants' quarters, over a corridor of communication between the kitchens and the grand staircase. When I returned to the Count's study, I overheard, before opening the door, my uncle pronouncing this judgment on me:

"'He may do wrong, for he has strong feelings, and we are all liable to honorable mistakes; but he has no vices.'

"'Well,' said the Count, with a kindly look, 'do you like yourself there? Tell me. There are so many rooms in this barrack that, if you were not comfortable, I could put you elsewhere.'

"'At my uncle's I had but one room,' replied I.

"'Well, you can settle yourself this evening,' said the Count, 'for your possessions, no doubt, are such as all students own, and a hackney coach will be enough to convey them. To-day we will all three dine together,' and he looked at my uncle.

"A splendid library opened from the Count's study, and he took us in there, showing me a pretty little recess decorated with paintings, which had formerly served, no doubt, as an oratory.

"'This is your cell,' said he. 'You will sit there when you have to work with me, for you will not be tethered by a chain;' and he explained in detail the kind and duration of my employment with him. As I listened I felt that he was a great political teacher.

"It took me about a month to familiarize myself with people and things, to learn the duties of my new office, and accustom myself to the Count's methods. A secretary necessarily watches the man who makes use of him. That man's tastes, passions, temper, and manias become the subject of involuntary study. The union of their two minds is at once more and less than a marriage.

"During these months the Count and I reciprocally studied each other. I learned with astonishment that Comte Octave was but thirty-seven years old. The merely superficial peacefulness of his life and the propriety of his conduct were the outcome not solely of a deep sense of duty and of stoical reflection; in my constant intercourse with this man—an extraordinary man to those who knew him well—I felt vast depths beneath his toil, beneath his acts of politeness, his mask of benignity, his assumption of resignation, which so closely resembled calmness that it is easy to mistake it. Just as when walking through forest-lands certain soils give forth under our feet a sound which enables us to guess whether they are dense masses of stone or a void; so intense egoism, though hidden under the flowers of politeness, and subterranean caverns eaten out by sorrow sound hollow under the constant touch of familiar life. It was sorrow and not despondency that dwelt in that really great soul. The Count had understood that actions, deeds, are the supreme law of social man. And he went on his way in spite of secret wounds, looking to the future with a tranquil eye, like a martyr full of faith.

"His concealed sadness, the bitter disenchantment from which he suffered, had not led him into philosophical deserts of incredulity; this brave statesman was religious, without ostentation; he always attended the earliest mass at

Saint-Paul's for pious workmen and servants. Not one of his friends, no one at Court, knew that he so punctually fulfilled the practice of religion. He was addicted to God as some men are addicted to a vice, with the greatest mystery. Thus one day I came to find the Count at the summit of an Alp of woe much higher than that on which many are who think themselves the most tried; who laugh at the passions and the beliefs of others because they have conquered their own; who play variations in every key of irony and disdain. He did not mock at those who still follow hope into the swamps whither she leads, nor those who climb a peak to be alone, nor those who persist in the fight, reddening the arena with their blood and strewing it with their illusions. He looked on the world as a whole; he mastered its beliefs; he listened to its complaining; he was doubtful of affection, and yet more of self-sacrifice; but this great and stern judge pitied them, or admired them, not with transient enthusiasm, but with silence, concentration, and the communion of a deeply-touched soul. He was a sort of catholic Manfred, and unstained by crime, carrying his choiceness into his faith, melting the snows by the fires of a sealed volcano, holding converse with a star seen by himself alone!

"I detected many dark riddles in his ordinary life. He evaded my gaze not like a traveler who, following a path, disappears from time to time in dells or ravines according to the formation of the soil, but like a sharpshooter who is being watched, who wants to hide himself, and seeks a cover. I could not account for his frequent absences at the times when he was working the hardest, and of which he made no secret from me, for he would say, 'Go on with this for me,' and trust me with the work in hand.

"This man, wrapped in the threefold duties of the statesman, the judge, and the orator, charmed me by a taste for flowers, which shows an elegant mind, and which is shared by almost all persons of refinement. His garden and his study were full of the rarest plants, but he always bought them half-withered. Perhaps it pleased him to see such an image of his own fate! He was faded like these dying flowers, whose almost decaying fragrance mounted strangely to his brain. The Count loved his country; he devoted himself to public interests with the frenzy of a heart that seeks to cheat some other passion; but the studies and work into which he threw himself were not enough for him; there were frightful struggles in his mind, of which some echoes reached me. Finally, he would give utterance to harrowing aspirations for happiness, and it seemed to me he ought yet to be happy; but what was the obstacle? Was there a woman he loved? This was a question I asked myself. You may imagine the extent of the circles of torment that my mind had searched before coming to so simple and so terrible a question. Notwithstanding his efforts, my patron did not succeed in stifling the movements of his heart. Under his austere manner, under the reserve of the magistrate, a passion rebelled, though coerced with such force that no one but I who lived with him ever guessed the secret. His motto seemed to be, 'I suffer, and am silent.' The escort of respect and admiration which attended him; the friendship of workers as valiant as himself—Grandville and Serizy, both presiding judges—had no hold over the Count: either he told them nothing, or they knew all. Impassible and lofty in public, the Count betrayed the man only on rare intervals when, alone in his garden or his study, he supposed himself unobserved; but then he was a child again, he gave course to the tears hidden beneath the toga, to the excitement which, if wrongly interpreted, might have damaged his credit for perspicacity as a statesman.

"When all this had become to me a matter of certainty, Comte Octave had all the attractions of a problem, and won on my affection as much as though he had been my own father. Can you enter into the feeling of curiosity, tempered by respect? What catastrophe had blasted this learned man, who, like Pitt, had devoted himself from the age of eighteen to the studies indispensable to power, while he had no ambition; this judge, who thoroughly knew the law of nations, political law, civil and criminal law, and who could find in these a weapon against every anxiety, against every mistake; this profound legislator, this serious writer, this pious celibate whose life sufficiently proved that he was open to no reproach? A criminal could not have been more hardly punished by God than was my master; sorrow had robbed him of half his slumbers; he never slept more than four hours. What struggle was it that went on in the depths of these hours apparently so calm, so studious, passing without a sound or a murmur, during which I often detected him, when the pen had dropped from his fingers, with his head resting on one hand, his eyes like two fixed stars, and sometimes wet with tears? How could the waters of that living spring flow over the burning strand without being dried up by the subterranean fire? Was there below it, as there is under the sea, between it and the central fires of the globe, a bed of granite? And would the volcano burst at last?

"Sometimes the Count would give me a look of that sagacious and keen-eyed curiosity by which one man searches another when he desires an accomplice; then he shunned my eye as he saw it open a mouth, so to speak, insisting on a reply, and seeming to say, 'Speak first!' Now and then Comte Octave's melancholy was surly and gruff. If these spurts of temper offended me, he could get over it without thinking of asking my pardon; but then his manners were gracious to the point of Christian humility.

"When I became attached like a son to this man—to me such a mystery, but so intelligible to the outer world, to whom the epithet eccentric is enough to account for all the enigmas of the heart—I changed the state of the house.

Neglect of his own interests was carried by the Count to the length of folly in the management of his affairs. Possessing an income of about a hundred and sixty thousand francs, without including the emoluments of his appointments —three of which did not come under the law against plurality—he spent sixty thousand, of which at least thirty thousand went to his servants. By the end of the first year I had got rid of all these rascals, and begged His Excellency to use his influence in helping me to get honest servants. By the end of the second year the Count, better fed and better served, enjoyed the comforts of modern life; he had fine horses, supplied by a coachman to whom I paid so much a month for each horse; his dinners on his reception days, furnished by Chevet at a price agreed upon, did him credit; his daily meals were prepared by an excellent cook found by my uncle, and helped by two kitchenmaids. The expenditure for housekeeping, not including purchases, was no more than thirty thousand francs a year; we had two additional men-servants, whose care restored the poetical aspect of the house; for this old palace, splendid even in its rust, had an air of dignity which neglect had dishonored.

"'I am no longer astonished,' said he, on hearing of these results, 'at the fortunes made by servants. In seven years I have had two cooks, who have become rich restaurant-keepers.'

"Early in the year 1826 the Count had, no doubt, ceased to watch me, and we were as closely attached as two men can be when one is subordinate to the other. He had never spoken to me of my future prospects, but he had taken an interest, both as a master and as a father, in training me. He often required me to collect materials for his most arduous labors; I drew up some of his reports, and he corrected them, showing the difference between his interpretation of the law, his views and mine. When at last I had produced a document which he could give in as his own he was delighted; this satisfaction was my reward, and he could see that I took it so. This little incident produced an extraordinary effect on a soul which seemed so stern. The Count pronounced sentence on me, to use a legal phrase, as supreme and royal judge; he took my head in his hands, and kissed me on the forehead.

"'Maurice,' he exclaimed, 'you are no longer my apprentice; I know not yet what you will be to me—but if no change occurs in my life, perhaps you will take the place of a son.'

"Comte Octave had introduced me to the best houses in Paris, whither I went in his stead, with his servants and carriage, on the too frequent occasions when, on the point of starting, he changed his mind, and sent for a hackney cab to take him—Where?—that was the mystery. By the welcome I met with I could judge of the Count's feelings towards me, and the earnestness of his recommendations. He supplied all my wants with the thoughtfulness of a father, and with all the greater liberality because my modesty left it to him always to think of me. Towards the end of January 1827, at the house of the Comtesse de Serizy, I had such persistent ill-luck at play that I lost two thousand francs, and I would not draw them out of my savings. Next morning I asked myself, 'Had I better ask my uncle for the money, or put my confidence in the Count?'

"I decided on the second alternative.

"'Yesterday,' said I, when he was at breakfast, 'I lost persistently at play; I was provoked, and went on; I owe two thousand francs. Will you allow me to draw the sum on account of my year's salary?'

"'No,' said he, with the sweetest smile; 'when a man plays in society, he must have a gambling purse. Draw six thousand francs; pay your debts. Henceforth we must go halves; for since you are my representative on most occasions, your self-respect must not be made to suffer for it.'

"I made no speech of thanks. Thanks would have been superfluous between us. This shade shows the character of our relations. And yet we had not yet unlimited confidence in each other; he did not open to me the vast subterranean chambers which I had detected in his secret life; and I, for my part, never said to him, 'What ails you? From what are you suffering?'

"What could he be doing during those long evenings? He would often come in on foot or in a hackney cab when I returned in a carriage—I, his secretary! Was so pious a man a prey to vices hidden under hypocrisy? Did he expend all the powers of his mind to satisfy a jealousy more dexterous than Othello's? Did he live with some woman unworthy of him? One morning, on returning from I have forgotten what shop, where I had just paid a bill, between the Church of Saint-Paul and the Hotel de Ville, I came across Comte Octave in such eager conversation with an old woman that he did not see me. The appearance of this hag filled me with strange suspicions, suspicions that were all the better founded because I never found that the Count invested his savings. Is it not shocking to think of? I was constituting myself my patron's censor. At that time I knew that he had more than six hundred thousand francs to invest; and if he had bought securities of any kind, his confidence in me was so complete in all that concerned his pecuniary interests, that I certainly should have known it.

"Sometimes, in the morning, the Count took exercise in his garden, to and fro, like a man to whom a walk is the hippogryph ridden by dreamy melancholy. He walked and walked! And he rubbed his hands enough to rub the skin off. And then, if I met him unexpectedly as he came to the angle of a path, I saw his face beaming. His eyes, instead of the hardness of a turquoise, had that velvety softness of the blue periwinkle, which had so much struck me on the occasion of my first visit, by reason of the astonishing contrast in the two different looks; the look of a happy man, and the look of an unhappy man. Two or three times at such a moment he had taken me by the arm and led me on; then he had said, 'What have you come to ask?' instead of pouring out his joy into my heart that opened to him. But more often, especially since I could do his work for him and write his reports, the unhappy man would sit for hours staring at the goldfish that swarmed in a handsome marble basin in the middle of the garden, round which grew an amphitheatre of the finest flowers. He, an accomplished statesman, seemed to have succeeded in making a passion of the mechanical amusement of crumbling bread to fishes.

"This is how the drama was disclosed of this second inner life, so deeply ravaged and storm-tossed, where, in a circle overlooked by Dante in his *Inferno*, horrible joys had their birth."

The Consul-General paused.

"On a certain Monday," he resumed, "as chance would have it, M. le President de Grandville and M. de Serizy (at that time Vice-President of the Council of State) had come to hold a meeting at Comte Octave's house. They formed a committee of three, of which I was the secretary. The Count had already got me the appointment of Auditor to the Council of State. All the documents requisite for their inquiry into the political matter privately submitted to these three gentlemen were laid out on one of the long tables in the library. MM. de Grandville and de Serizy had trusted to the Count to make the preliminary examination of the papers relating to the matter. To avoid the necessity for carrying all the papers to M. de Serizy, as president of the commission, it was decided that they should meet first in the Rue Payenne. The Cabinet at the Tuileries attached great importance to this piece of work, of which the chief burden fell on me—and to which I owed my appointment, in the course of that year, to be Master of Appeals.

"Though the Comtes de Grandville and de Serizy, whose habits were much the same as my patron's, never dined away from home, we were still discussing the matter at a late hour, when we were startled by the man-servant calling me aside to say, 'MM. the Cures of Saint-Paul and of the White Friars have been waiting in the drawing-room for two hours.'

"It was nine o'clock.

"'Well, gentlemen, you find yourselves compelled to dine with priests,' said Comte Octave to his colleagues. 'I do not know whether Grandville can overcome his horror of a priest's gown——'

"'It depends on the priest.'

"'One of them is my uncle, and the other is the Abbe Gaudron,' said I. 'Do not be alarmed; the Abbe Fontanon is no longer second priest at Saint-Paul ____'

"'Well, let us dine,' replied the President de Grandville. 'A bigot frightens me, but there is no one so cheerful as a truly pious man.'

"We went into the drawing-room. The dinner was delightful. Men of real information, politicians to whom business gives both consummate experience and the practice of speech, are admirable story-tellers, when they tell stories. With them there is no medium; they are either heavy, or they are sublime. In this delightful sport Prince Metternich is as good as Charles Nodier. The fun of a statesman, cut in facets like a diamond, is sharp, sparkling, and full of sense. Being sure that the proprieties would be observed by these three superior men, my uncle allowed his wit full play, a refined wit, gentle, penetrating, and elegant, like that of all men who are accustomed to conceal their thoughts under the black robe. And you may rely upon it, there was nothing vulgar nor idle in this light talk, which I would compare, for its effect on the soul, to Rossini's music.

"The Abbe Gaudron was, as M. de Grandville said, a Saint Peter rather than a Saint Paul, a peasant full of faith, as square on his feet as he was tall, a sacerdotal of whose ignorance in matters of the world and of literature enlivened the conversation by guileless amazement and unexpected questions. They came to talking of one of the plague spots of social life, of which we were just now speaking—adultery. My uncle remarked on the contradiction which the legislators of the Code, still feeling the blows of the revolutionary storm, had established between civil and religious law, and which he said was at the root of all the mischief.

"'In the eyes of the Church,' said he, 'adultery is a crime; in those of your tribunals it is a misdemeanor. Adultery drives to the police court in a carriage instead of standing at the bar to be tried. Napoleon's Council of State, touched with tenderness towards erring women, was quite inefficient. Ought they not in this case to have harmonized the civil and the religious law, and have sent the guilty wife to a convent, as of old?'

"'To a convent!' said M. de Serizy. 'They must first have created convents, and in those days monasteries were being turned into barracks. Besides, think of what you say, M. l'Abbe—give to God what society would have none of?'

"'Oh!' said the Comte de Grandville, 'you do not know France. They were obliged to leave the husband free to take proceedings: well, there are not ten cases of adultery brought up in a year.'

"'M. l'Abbe preaches for his own saint, for it was Jesus Christ who invented adultery,' said Comte Octave. 'In the East, the cradle of the human race, woman was merely a luxury, and there was regarded as a chattel; no virtues were demanded of her but obedience and beauty. By exalting the soul above the body, the modern family in Europe—a daughter of Christ—invented indissoluble marriage, and made it a sacrament.'

"'Ah! the Church saw the difficulties,' exclaimed M. de Grandville.

"'This institution has given rise to a new world,' the Count went on with a smile. 'But the practices of that world will never be that of a climate where women are marriageable at seven years of age, and more than old at five-and-twenty. The Catholic Church overlooked the needs of half the globe.—So let us discuss Europe only.

"'Is woman our superior or our inferior? That is the real question so far as we are concerned. If woman is our inferior, by placing her on so high a level as the Church does, fearful punishments for adultery were needful. And formerly that was what was done. The cloister or death sums up early legislation. But since then practice has modified the law, as is always the case. The throne served as a hotbed for adultery, and the increase of this inviting crime marks the decline of the dogmas of the Catholic Church. In these days, in cases where the Church now exacts no more than sincere repentance from the erring wife, society is satisfied with a brand-mark instead of an execution. The law still condemns the guilty, but it no longer terrifies them. In short, there are two standards of morals: that of the world, and that of the Code. Where the Code is weak, as I admit with our dear Abbe, the world is audacious and satirical. There are so few judges who would not gladly have committed the fault against which they hurl the rather stolid thunders of their "Inasmuch." The world, which gives the lie to the law alike in its rejoicings, in its habits, and in its pleasures, is severer than the Code and the Church; the world punishes a blunder after encouraging hypocrisy. The whole economy of the law on marriage seems to me to require reconstruction from the bottom to the top. The French law would be perfect perhaps if it excluded daughters from inheriting.'

"'We three among us know the question very thoroughly,' said the Comte de Grandville with a laugh. 'I have a wife I cannot live with. Serizy has a wife who will not live with him. As for you, Octave, yours ran away from you. So we three represent every case of the conjugal conscience, and, no doubt, if ever divorce is brought in again, we shall form the committee.'

"Octave's fork dropped on his glass, broke it, and broke his plate. He had turned as pale as death, and flashed a thunderous glare at M. de Grandville, by which he hinted at my presence, and which I caught.

20

"'Forgive me, my dear fellow. I did not see Maurice,' the President went on. 'Serizy and I, after being the witnesses to your marriage, became your accomplices; I did not think I was committing an indiscretion in the presence of these two venerable priests.'

"M. de Serizy changed the subject by relating all he had done to please his wife without ever succeeding. The old man concluded that it was impossible to regulate human sympathies and antipathies; he maintained that social law was never more perfect than when it was nearest to natural law. Now Nature takes no account of the affinities of souls; her aim is fulfilled by the propagation of the species. Hence, the Code, in its present form, was wise in leaving a wide latitude to chance. The incapacity of daughters to inherit so long as there were male heirs was an excellent provision, whether to hinder the degeneration of the race, or to make households happier by abolishing scandalous unions and giving the sole preference to moral qualities and beauty.

"'But then,' he exclaimed, lifting his hand with a gesture of disgust, 'how are we to perfect legislation in a country which insists on bringing together seven or eight hundred legislators!—After all, if I am sacrificed,' he added, 'I have a child to succeed me.'

"'Setting aside all the religious question,' my uncle said, 'I would remark to your Excellency that Nature only owes us life, and that it is society that owes us happiness. Are you a father?' asked my uncle.

"'And I—have I any children?' said Comte Octave in a hollow voice, and his tone made such an impression that there was no more talk of wives or marriage.

"When coffee had been served, the two Counts and the two priests stole away, seeing that poor Octave had fallen into a fit of melancholy which prevented his noticing their disappearance. My patron was sitting in an armchair by the fire, in the attitude of a man crushed.

"'You now know the secret of my life, said he to me on noticing that we were alone. 'After three years of married life, one evening when I came in I found a letter in which the Countess announced her flight. The letter did not lack dignity, for it is in the nature of women to preserve some virtues even when committing that horrible sin.—The story is now that my wife went abroad in a ship that was wrecked; she is supposed to be dead. I have lived alone for seven years!—Enough for this evening, Maurice. We will talk of my situation when I have grown used to the idea of speaking of it to you. When we suffer from a chronic disease, it needs time to become accustomed to improvement. That improvement often seems to be merely another aspect of the complaint.'

"I went to bed greatly agitated; for the mystery, far from being explained, seemed to me more obscure than ever. I foresaw some strange drama indeed, for I understood that there could be no vulgar difference between the woman that Count could choose and such a character as his. The events which had driven the Countess to leave a man so noble, so amiable, so perfect, so loving, so worthy to be loved, must have been singular, to say the least. M. de Grandville's remark had been like a torch flung into the caverns over which I had so long been walking; and though the flame lighted them but dimly, my eyes could perceive their wide extent! I could imagine the Count's sufferings without knowing their depths or their bitterness. That sallow face, those parched temples, those overwhelming studies, those moments of absentmindedness, the smallest details of the life of this married bachelor, all stood out in luminous relief during the hour of mental questioning, which is, as it were, the twilight before sleep, and to which any man would have given himself up, as I did.

"Oh! how I loved my poor master! He seemed to me sublime. I read a poem of melancholy, I saw perpetual activity in the heart I had accused of being torpid. Must not supreme grief always come at last to stagnation? Had this judge, who had so much in his power, ever revenged himself? Was he feeding himself on her long agony? Is it not a remarkable thing in Paris to keep anger always seething for ten years? What had Octave done since this great misfortune—for the separation of husband and wife is a great misfortune in our day, when domestic life has become a social question, which it never was of old?

"We allowed a few days to pass on the watch, for great sorrows have a diffidence of their own; but at last, one evening, the Count said in a grave voice:

"'Stay.'

"This, as nearly as may be, is his story.

"'My father had a ward, rich and lovely, who was sixteen at the time when I came back from college to live in this old house. Honorine, who had been brought up by my mother, was just awakening to life. Full of grace and of childish ways, she dreamed of happiness as she would have dreamed of jewels; perhaps happiness seemed to her the jewel of the soul. Her piety was not free from puerile pleasures; for everything, even religion, was poetry to her ingenuous heart. She looked to the future as a perpetual fete. Innocent and pure, no delirium had disturbed her dream. Shame and grief had never tinged her cheek nor moistened her eye. She did not even inquire into the secret of her involuntary emotions on a fine spring day. And then, she felt that she was weak and destined to obedience, and she awaited marriage without wishing for it. Her smiling imagination knew nothing of the corruption—necessary perhaps—which literature imparts by depicting the passions; she knew nothing of the world, and was ignorant of all the dangers of society. The dear child had suffered so little that she had not even developed her courage. In short, her guilelessness would have led her to walk fearless among serpents, like the ideal figure of Innocence a painter once created. We lived together like two brothers.

"'At the end of a year I said to her one day, in the garden of this house, by the basin, as we stood throwing crumbs to the fish:

"""Would you like that we should be married? With me you could do whatever you please, while another man would make you unhappy."

"""Mamma," said she to my mother, who came out to join us, "Octave and I have agreed to be married——"

"""What! at seventeen?" said my mother. "No, you must wait eighteen months; and if eighteen months hence you like each other, well, your birth and fortunes are equal, you can make a marriage which is suitable, as well as being a love match."

"'When I was six-and-twenty, and Honorine nineteen, we were married. Our respect for my father and mother, old folks of the Bourbon Court, hindered us from making this house fashionable, or renewing the furniture; we lived on, as we had done in the past, as children. However, I went into society; I initiated my wife into the world of fashion; and I regarded it as one of my duties to instruct her.

"'I recognized afterwards that marriages contracted under such circumstances as ours bear in themselves a rock against which many affections are wrecked, many prudent calculations, many lives. The husband becomes a pedagogue, or, if you like, a professor, and love perishes under the rod which, sooner or later, gives pain; for a young and handsome wife, at once discreet and laughter-loving, will not accept any superiority above that with which she is endowed by nature. Perhaps I was in the wrong? During the difficult beginnings of a household I, perhaps, assumed a magisterial tone? On the other hand, I may have made the mistake of trusting too entirely to that artless nature; I kept no watch over the Countess, in whom revolt seemed to me impossible? Alas! neither in politics nor in domestic life has it yet been ascertained whether empires and happiness are wrecked by too much confidence or too much severity! Perhaps again, the husband failed to realize Honorine's girlish dreams? Who can tell, while happy days last, what precepts he has neglected?'

"I remember only the broad outlines of the reproaches the Count addressed to himself, with all the good faith of an anatomist seeking the cause of a disease which might be overlooked by his brethren; but his merciful indulgence struck me then as really worthy of that of Jesus Christ when He rescued the woman taken in adultery.

"'It was eighteen months after my father's death—my mother followed him to the tomb in a few months—when the fearful night came which surprised me by Honorine's farewell letter. What poetic delusion had seduced my wife? Was it through her senses? Was it the magnetism of misfortune or of genius? Which of these powers had taken her by storm or misled her?—I would not know. The blow was so terrible, that for a month I remained stunned. Afterwards, reflection counseled me to continue in ignorance, and Honorine's misfortunes have since taught me too much about all these things.—So far, Maurice, the story is commonplace enough; but one word will change it all: I love Honorine, I have never ceased to worship her. From the day when she left me I have lived on memory; one by one I recall the pleasures for which Honorine no doubt had no taste.

"'Oh!' said he, seeing the amazement in my eyes, 'do not make a hero of me, do not think me such a fool, as the Colonel of the Empire would say, as to have sought no diversion. Alas, my boy! I was either too young or too much in love; I have not in the whole world met with another woman. After frightful struggles with myself, I tried to forget; money in hand, I stood on the very threshold of infidelity, but there the memory of Honorine rose before me like a white statue. As I recalled the infinite delicacy of that exquisite skin, through which the blood might be seen coursing and the nerves quivering; as I saw in fancy that ingenuous face, as guileless on the eve of my sorrows as on the day when I said to her, "Shall we marry?" as I remembered a heavenly fragrance, the very odor of virtue, and the light in her eyes, the prettiness of her movements, I fled like a man preparing to violate a tomb, who sees emerging from it the transfigured soul of the dead. At consultations, in Court, by night, I dream so incessantly of Honorine that only by excessive strength of mind do I succeed in attending to what I am doing and saying. This is the secret of my labors.

"'Well, I felt no more anger with her than a father can feel on seeing his beloved child in some danger it has imprudently rushed into. I understood that I had made a poem of my wife—a poem I delighted in with such intoxication, that I fancied she shared the intoxication. Ah! Maurice, an indiscriminating passion in a husband is a mistake that may lead to any crime in a wife. I had no doubt left all the faculties of this child, loved as a child, entirely unemployed; I had perhaps wearied her with my love before the hour of loving had struck for her! Too young to understand that in the constancy of the wife lies the germ of the mother's devotion, she mistook this first test of marriage for life itself, and the refractory child cursed life, unknown to me, nor daring to complain to me, out of sheer modesty perhaps! In so cruel a position she would be defenceless against any man who stirred her deeply.— And I, so wise a judge as they say—I, who have a kind heart, but whose mind was absorbed—I understood too late these unwritten laws of the woman's code, I read them by the light of the fire that wrecked my roof. Then I constituted my heart a tribunal by virtue of the law, for the law makes the husband a judge: I acquitted my wife, and I condemned myself. But love took possession of me as a passion, the mean, despotic passion which comes over some old men. At this day I love the absent Honorine as a man of sixty loves a woman whom he must possess at any cost, and yet I feel the strength of a young man. I have the insolence of the old man and the reserve of a boy.— My dear fellow, society only laughs at such a desperate conjugal predicament. Where it pities a lover, it regards a husband as ridiculously inept; it makes sport of those who cannot keep the woman they have secured under the canopy of the Church, and before the Maire's scarf of office. And I had to keep silence.

"'Serizy is happy. His indulgence allows him to see his wife; he can protect and defend her; and, as he adores her, he knows all the perfect joys of a benefactor whom nothing can disturb, not even ridicule, for he pours it himself on his fatherly pleasures. "I remain married only for my wife's sake," he said to me one day on coming out of court.

"'But I—I have nothing; I have not even to face ridicule, I who live solely on a love which is starving! I who can never find a word to say to a woman of the world! I who loathe prostitution! I who am faithful under a spell!—But for my religious faith, I should have killed myself. I have defied the gulf of hard work; I have thrown myself into it, and come out again alive, fevered, burning, bereft of sleep!——'

"I cannot remember all the words of this eloquent man, to whom passion gave an eloquence indeed so far above that of the pleader that, as I listened to him, I, like him, felt my cheeks wet with tears. You may conceive of my feelings when, after a pause, during which we dried them away, he finished his story with this revelation:—

"'This is the drama of my soul, but it is not the actual living drama which is at this moment being acted in Paris! The interior drama interests nobody. I know it; and you will one day admit that it is so, you, who at this moment shed tears with me; no one can burden his heart or his skin with another's

25

pain. The measure of our sufferings is in ourselves.—You even understand my sorrows only by very vague analogy. Could you see me calming the most violent frenzy of despair by the contemplation of a miniature in which I can see and kiss her brow, the smile on her lips, the shape of her face, can breathe the whiteness of her skin; which enables me almost to feel, to play with the black masses of her curling hair?—Could you see me when I leap with hope —when I writhe under the myriad darts of despair—when I tramp through the mire of Paris to quell my irritation by fatigue? I have fits of collapse comparable to those of a consumptive patient, moods of wild hilarity, terrors as of a murderer who meets a sergeant of police. In short, my life is a continual paroxysm of fears, joy, and dejection.

"'As to the drama—it is this. You imagine that I am occupied with the Council of State, the Chamber, the Courts, Politics.—Why, dear me, seven hours at night are enough for all that, so much are my faculties overwrought by the life I lead! Honorine is my real concern. To recover my wife is my only study; to guard her in her cage, without her suspecting that she is in my power; to satisfy her needs, to supply the little pleasure she allows herself, to be always about her like a sylph without allowing her to see or to suspect me, for if she did, the future would be lost,—that is my life, my true life.—For seven years I have never gone to bed without going first to see the light of her night-lamp, or her shadow on the window curtains.

"'She left my house, choosing to take nothing but the dress she wore that day. The child carried her magnanimity to the point of folly! Consequently, eighteen months after her flight she was deserted by her lover, who was appalled by the cold, cruel, sinister, and revolting aspect of poverty—the coward! The man had, no doubt, counted on the easy and luxurious life in Switzerland or Italy which fine ladies indulge in when they leave their husbands. Honorine has sixty thousand francs a year of her own. The wretch left the dear creature expecting an infant, and without a penny. In the month of November 1820 I found means to persuade the best *accoucheur* in Paris to play the part of a humble suburban apothecary. I induced the priest of the parish in which the Countess was living to supply her needs as though he were performing an act of charity. Then to hide my wife, to secure her against discovery, to find her a housekeeper who would be devoted to me and be my intelligent confidante—it was a task worthy of Figaro! You may suppose that to discover where my wife had taken refuge I had only to make up my mind to it.

"'After three months of desperation rather than despair, the idea of devoting myself to Honorine with God only in my secret, was one of those poems which occur only to the heart of a lover through life and death! Love must have its daily food. And ought I not to protect this child, whose guilt was the outcome of my imprudence, against fresh disaster—to fulfil my part, in short, as a guardian angel?—At the age of seven months her infant died, happily for her and for me. For nine months more my wife lay between life and death, deserted at the time when she most needed a manly arm; but this arm,' said he, holding out his own with a gesture of angelic dignity, 'was extended over her head. Honorine was nursed as she would have been in her own home. When, on her recovery, she asked how and by whom she had been assisted, she was told—"By the Sisters of Charity in the neighborhood—by the Maternity Society—by the parish priest, who took an interest in her."

"'This woman, whose pride amounts to a vice, has shown a power of resistance in misfortune, which on some evenings I call the obstinacy of a mule. Honorine was bent on earning her living. My wife works! For five years past I have lodged her in the Rue Saint-Maur, in a charming little house, where she makes artificial flowers and articles of fashion. She believes that she sells the product of her elegant fancywork to a shop, where she is so well paid that she makes twenty francs a day, and in these six years she had never had a moment's suspicion. She pays for everything she needs at about the third of its value, so that on six thousand francs a year she lives as if she had fifteen thousand. She is devoted to flowers, and pays a hundred crowns to a gardener, who costs me twelve hundred in wages, and sends me in a bill for two thousand francs every three months. I have promised the man a market-garden with a house on it close to the porter's lodge in the Rue Saint-Maur. I hold this ground in the name of a clerk of the law courts. The smallest indiscretion would ruin the gardener's prospects. Honorine has her little house, a garden, and a splendid hothouse, for a rent of five hundred francs a year. There she lives under the name of her housekeeper, Madame Gobain, the old woman of impeccable discretion whom I was so lucky as to find, and whose affection Honorine has won. But her zeal, like that of the gardener, is kept hot by the promise of reward at the moment of success. The porter and his wife cost me dreadfully dear for the same reasons. However, for three years Honorine has been happy, believing that she owes to her own toil all the luxury of flowers, dress, and comfort.

"'Oh! I know what you are about to say,' cried the Count, seeing a question in my eyes and on my lips. 'Yes, yes; I have made the attempt. My wife was formerly living in the Faubourg Saint-Antoine. One day when, from what Gobain told me, I believed in some chance of a reconciliation, I wrote by post a letter, in which I tried to propitiate my wife—a letter written and re-written twenty times! I will not describe my agonies. I went from the Rue Payenne to the Rue de Reuilly like a condemned wretch going from the Palais de Justice to his execution, but he goes on a cart, and I was on foot. It was dark—there was a fog; I went to meet Madame Gobain, who was to come and tell me what my wife had done. Honorine, on recognizing my writing, had thrown the letter into the fire without reading it.—"Madame Gobain," she had exclaimed, "I leave this to-morrow."

"'What a dagger-stroke was this to a man who found inexhaustible pleasure in the trickery by which he gets the finest Lyons velvet at twelve francs a yard, a pheasant, a fish, a dish of fruit, for a tenth of their value, for a woman so ignorant as to believe that she is paying ample wages with two hundred and fifty francs to Madame Gobain, a cook fit for a bishop.

"'You have sometimes found me rubbing my hands in the enjoyment of a sort of happiness. Well, I had just succeeded in some ruse worthy of the stage. I had just deceived my wife—I had sent her by a purchaser of wardrobes an Indian shawl, to be offered to her as the property of an actress who had hardly worn it, but in which I—the solemn lawyer whom you know—had wrapped myself for a night! In short, my life at this day may be summed up in the two words which express the extremes of torment—I love, and I wait! I have in Madame Gobain a faithful spy on the heart I worship. I go every evening to chat with the old woman, to hear from her all that Honorine has done during the day, the lightest word she has spoken, for a single exclamation might betray to me the secrets of that soul which is wilfully deaf and dumb. Honorine is pious; she attends the Church services and prays, but she has never been to confession or taken the Communion; she foresees what a priest would tell her. She will not listen to the advice, to the injunction, that she should return to me. This horror of me overwhelms me, dismays me, for I have never done her the smallest harm. I have always been kind to her. Granting even that I may have been a little hasty when teaching her, that my man's irony may have hurt her legitimate girlish pride, is that a reason for persisting in a determination which only the most implacable hatred could have inspired? Honorine has never told Madame Gobain who she is; she keeps absolute silence as to her marriage, so that the worthy and respectable woman can never speak a word in my favor, for she is the only person in the house who knows my secret. The others know nothing; they live under the awe caused by the name of the Prefect of Police, and their respect for the power of a Minister. Hence it is impossible for me to penetrate that heart; the citadel is mine, but I cannot get into it. I have not a single means of action. An act of violence would ruin me for ever.

"'How can I argue against reasons of which I know nothing? Should I write a letter, and have it copied by a public writer, and laid before Honorine? But that would be to run the risk of a third removal. The last cost me fifty thousand francs. The purchase was made in the first instance in the name of the secretary whom you succeeded. The unhappy man, who did not know how lightly I sleep, was detected by me in the act of opening a box in which I had put the private agreement; I coughed, and he was seized with a panic; next day I compelled him to sell the house to the man in whose name it now stands, and I turned him out.

"'If it were not that I feel all my noblest faculties as a man satisfied, happy, expansive; if the part I am playing were not that of divine fatherhood; if I did not drink in delight by every pore, there are moments when I should believe that I was a monomaniac. Sometimes at night I hear the jingling bells of madness. I dread the violent transitions from a feeble hope, which sometimes shines and flashes up, to complete despair, falling as low as man can fall. A few days since I was seriously considering the horrible end of the story of Lovelace and Clarissa Harlowe, and saying to myself, if Honorine were the mother of a child of mine, must she not necessarily return under her husband's roof?

"'And I have such complete faith in a happy future, that ten months ago I bought and paid for one of the handsomest houses in the Faubourg Saint-Honore. If I win back Honorine, I will not allow her to see this house again, nor the room from which she fled. I mean to place my idol in a new temple, where she may feel that life is altogether new. That house is being made a marvel of elegance and taste. I have been told of a poet who, being almost mad with love for an actress, bought the handsomest bed in Paris without knowing how the actress would reward his passion. Well, one of the coldest of lawyers, a man who is supposed to be the gravest adviser of the Crown, was stirred to the depths of his heart by that anecdote. The orator of the Legislative Chamber can understand the poet who fed his ideal on material possibilities. Three days before the arrival of Maria Louisa, Napoleon flung himself on his wedding bed at Compiegne. All stupendous passions have the same impulses. I love as a poet—as an emperor!'

"As I heard the last words, I believed that Count Octave's fears were realized; he had risen, and was walking up and down, and gesticulating, but he stopped as if shocked by the vehemence of his own words.

"'I am very ridiculous,' he added, after a long pause, looking at me, as if craving a glance of pity.

"'No, monsieur, you are very unhappy.'

"'Ah yes!' said he, taking up the thread of his confidences. 'From the violence of my speech you may, you must believe in the intensity of a physical passion which for nine years has absorbed all my faculties; but that is nothing in comparison with the worship I feel for the soul, the mind, the heart, all in that woman; the enchanting divinities in the train of Love, with whom we pass our life, and who form the daily poem of a fugitive delight. By a phenomenon of retrospection I see now the graces of Honorine's mind and heart, to which I paid little heed in the time of my happiness—like all who are happy. From day to day I have appreciated the extent of my loss, discovering the exquisite gifts of that capricious and refractory young creature who has grown so strong and so proud under the heavy hand of poverty and the shock of the most cowardly desertion. And that heavenly blossom is fading in solitude and hiding!—Ah! The law of which we were speaking,' he went on with bitter irony, 'the law is a squad of gendarmes—my wife seized and dragged away by force! Would not that be to triumph over a corpse? Religion has no hold on her; she craves its poetry, she prays, but she does not listen to the commandments of the Church. I, for my part, have exhausted everything in the way of mercy, of kindness, of love; I am at my wits' end. Only one chance of victory is left to me; the cunning and patience with which bird-catchers at last entrap the wariest birds, the swiftest, the most capricious, and the rarest. Hence, Maurice, when M. de Grandville's indiscretion betrayed to you the secret of my life, I ended by regarding this incident as one of the decrees of fate, one of the utterances for which gamblers listen and pray in the midst of their most impassioned play…. Have you enough affection for me to show me romantic devotion?'

"'I see what you are coming to, Monsieur le Comte,' said I, interrupting him; 'I guess your purpose. Your first secretary tried to open your deed box. I know the heart of your second—he might fall in love with your wife. And can you devote him to destruction by sending him into the fire? Can any one put his hand into a brazier without burning it?'

"'You are a foolish boy,' replied the Count. 'I will send you well gloved. It is no secretary of mine that will be lodged in the Rue Saint-Maur in the little garden-house which I have at his disposal. It is my distant cousin, Baron de l'Hostal, a lawyer high in office…'"

"After a moment of silent surprise, I heard the gate bell ring, and a carriage came into the courtyard. Presently the footman announced Madame de Courteville and her daughter. The Count had a large family connection on his mother's side. Madame de Courteville, his cousin, was the widow of a judge on the bench of the Seine division, who had left her a daughter and no fortune whatever. What could a woman of nine-and-twenty be in comparison with a young girl of twenty, as lovely as imagination could wish for an ideal mistress?

"'Baron, and Master of Appeals, till you get something better, and this old house settled on her,—would not you have enough good reasons for not falling in love with the Countess?' he said to me in a whisper, as he took me by the hand and introduced me to Madame de Courteville and her daughter.

"I was dazzled, not so much by these advantages of which I had never dreamed, but by Amelie de Courteville, whose beauty was thrown into relief by one of those well-chosen toilets which a mother can achieve for a daughter when she wants to see her married.

"But I will not talk of myself," said the Consul after a pause.

"Three weeks later I went to live in the gardener's cottage, which had been cleaned, repaired, and furnished with the celerity which is explained by three words: Paris; French workmen; money! I was as much in love as the Count could possibly desire as a security. Would the prudence of a young man of five-and-twenty be equal to the part I was undertaking, involving a friend's happiness? To settle that matter, I may confess that I counted very much on my uncle's advice; for I had been authorized by the Count to take him into confidence in any case where I deemed his interference necessary. I engaged a garden; I devoted myself to horticulture; I worked frantically, like a man whom nothing can divert, turning up the soil of the market-garden, and appropriating the ground to the culture of flowers. Like the maniacs of England, or of Holland, I gave it out that I was devoted to one kind of flower, and especially grew dahlias, collecting every variety. You will understand that my conduct, even in the smallest details, was laid down for me by the Count, whose whole intellectual powers were directed to the most trifling incidents of the tragi-comedy enacted in the Rue Saint-Maur. As soon as the Countess had gone to bed, at about eleven at night, Octave, Madame Gobain, and I sat in council. I heard the old woman's report to the Count of his wife's least proceedings during the day. He inquired into everything: her meals, her occupations, her frame of mind, her plans for the morrow, the flowers she proposed to imitate. I understood what love in despair may be when it is the threefold passion of the heart, the mind, and the senses. Octave lived only for that hour.

"During two months, while my work in the garden lasted, I never set eyes on the little house where my fair neighbor dwelt. I had not even inquired whether I had a neighbor, though the Countess' garden was divided from mine by a paling, along which she had planted cypress trees already four feet high. One fine morning Madame Gobain announced to her mistress, as a disastrous piece of news, the intention, expressed by an eccentric creature who had become her neighbor, of building a wall between the two gardens, at the end of the year. I will say nothing of the curiosity which consumed me to see the Countess! The wish almost extinguished my budding love for Amelie de Courteville. My scheme for building a wall was indeed a dangerous threat. There would be no more fresh air for Honorine, whose garden would then be a sort of narrow alley shut in between my wall and her own little house. This dwelling, formerly a summer villa, was like a house of cards; it was not more than thirty feet deep, and about a hundred feet long. The garden front, painted in the German fashion, imitated a trellis with flowers up to the second floor, and was really a charming example of the Pompadour style, so well called rococo. A long avenue of limes led up to it. The gardens of the pavilion and my plot of ground were in the shape of a hatchet, of which this avenue was the handle. My wall would cut away three-quarters of the hatchet.

"The Countess was in despair.

"'My good Gobain,' said she, 'what sort of man is this florist?'

"'On my word,' said the housekeeper, 'I do not know whether it will be possible to tame him. He seems to have a horror of women. He is the nephew of a Paris cure. I have seen the uncle but once; a fine old man of sixty, very ugly, but very amiable. It is quite possible that this priest encourages his nephew, as they say in the neighborhood, in his love of flowers, that nothing worse may happen——'

"'Why—what?'

"'Well, your neighbor is a little cracked!' said Gobain, tapping her head!

"Now a harmless lunatic is the only man whom no woman ever distrusts in the matter of sentiment. You will see how wise the Count had been in choosing this disguise for me.

"'What ails him then?' asked the Countess.

"'He has studied too hard,' replied Gobain; 'he has turned misanthropic. And he has his reasons for disliking women—well, if you want to know all that is said about him——'

"'Well,' said Honorine, 'madmen frighten me less than sane folks; I will speak to him myself! Tell him that I beg him to come here. If I do not succeed, I will send for the cure.'

"The day after this conversation, as I was walking along my graveled path, I caught sight of the half-opened curtains on the first floor of the little house, and of a woman's face curiously peeping out. Madame Gobain called me. I hastily glanced at the Countess' house, and by a rude shrug expressed, 'What do I care for your mistress!'

"'Madame,' said Gobain, called upon to give an account of her errand, 'the madman bid me leave him in peace, saying that even a charcoal seller is master in his own premises, especially when he has no wife.'

"'He is perfectly right,' said the Countess.

"'Yes, but he ended by saying, "I will go," when I told him that he would greatly distress a lady living in retirement, who found her greatest solace in growing flowers.'

"Next day a signal from Gobain informed me that I was expected. After the Countess' breakfast, when she was walking to and fro in front of her house, I broke out some palings and went towards her. I had dressed myself like a countryman, in an old pair of gray flannel trousers, heavy wooden shoes, and shabby shooting coat, a peaked cap on my head, a ragged bandana round my neck, hands soiled with mould, and a dibble in my hand.

33

"'Madame,' said the housekeeper, 'this good man is your neighbor.'

"The Countess was not alarmed. I saw at last the woman whom her own conduct and her husband's confidences had made me so curious to meet. It was in the early days of May. The air was pure, the weather serene; the verdure of the first foliage, the fragrance of spring formed a setting for this creature of sorrow. As I then saw Honorine I understood Octave's passion and the truthfulness of his description, 'A heavenly flower!'

"Her pallor was what first struck me by its peculiar tone of white—for there are as many tones of white as of red or blue. On looking at the Countess, the eye seemed to feel that tender skin, where the blood flowed in the blue veins. At the slightest emotion the blood mounted under the surface in rosy flushes like a cloud. When we met, the sunshine, filtering through the light foliage of the acacias, shed on Honorine the pale gold, ambient glory in which Raphael and Titian, alone of all painters, have been able to enwrap the Virgin. Her brown eyes expressed both tenderness and vivacity; their brightness seemed reflected in her face through the long downcast lashes. Merely by lifting her delicate eyelids, Honorine could cast a spell; there was so much feeling, dignity, terror, or contempt in her way of raising or dropping those veils of the soul. She could freeze or give life by a look. Her light-brown hair, carelessly knotted on her head, outlined a poet's brow, high, powerful, and dreamy. The mouth was wholly voluptuous. And to crown all by a grace, rare in France, though common in Italy, all the lines and forms of the head had a stamp of nobleness which would defy the outrages of time.

"Though slight, Honorine was not thin, and her figure struck me as being one that might revive love when it believed itself exhausted. She perfectly represented the idea conveyed by the word *mignonne*, for she was one of those pliant little women who allow themselves to be taken up, petted, set down, and taken up again like a kitten. Her small feet, as I heard them on the gravel, made a light sound essentially their own, that harmonized with the rustle of her dress, producing a feminine music which stamped itself on the heart, and remained distinct from the footfall of a thousand other women. Her gait bore all the quarterings of her race with so much pride, that, in the street, the least respectful working man would have made way for her. Gay and tender, haughty and imposing, it was impossible to understand her, excepting as gifted with these apparently incompatible qualities, which, nevertheless, had left her still a child. But it was a child who might be as strong as an angel; and, like the angel, once hurt in her nature, she would be implacable.

"Coldness on that face must no doubt be death to those on whom her eyes had smiled, for whom her set lips had parted, for those whose soul had drunk in the melody of that voice, lending to her words the poetry of song by its

34

peculiar intonation. Inhaling the perfume of violets that accompanied her, I understood how the memory of this wife had arrested the Count on the threshold of debauchery, and how impossible it would be ever to forget a creature who really was a flower to the touch, a flower to the eye, a flower of fragrance, a heavenly flower to the soul.... Honorine inspired devotion, chivalrous devotion, regardless of reward. A man on seeing her must say to himself:

"'Think, and I will divine your thought; speak, and I will obey. If my life, sacrificed in torments, can procure you one day's happiness, take my life, I will smile like a martyr at the stake, for I shall offer that day to God, as a token to which a father responds on recognizing a gift to his child.' Many women study their expression, and succeed in producing effects similar to those which would have struck you at first sight of the Countess; only, in her, it was all the outcome of a delightful nature, that inimitable nature went at once to the heart. If I tell you all this, it is because her soul, her thoughts, the exquisiteness of her heart, are all we are concerned with, and you would have blamed me if I had not sketched them for you.

"I was very near forgetting my part as a half-crazy lout, clumsy, and by no means chivalrous.

"'I am told, madame, that you are fond of flowers?'

"'I am an artificial flower-maker,' said she. 'After growing flowers, I imitate them, like a mother who is artist enough to have the pleasure of painting her children.... That is enough to tell you that I am poor and unable to pay for the concession I am anxious to obtain from you?'

"'But how,' said I, as grave as a judge, 'can a lady of such rank as yours would seem to be, ply so humble a calling? Have you, like me, good reasons for employing your fingers so as to keep your brains from working?'

"'Let us stick to the question of the wall,' said she, with a smile.

"'Why, we have begun at the foundations,' said I. 'Must not I know which of us ought to yield to the other in behalf of our suffering, or, if you choose, of our mania?—Oh! what a charming clump of narcissus! They are as fresh as this spring morning!'

"I assure you, she had made for herself a perfect museum of flowers and shrubs, which none might see but the sun, and of which the arrangement had been prompted by the genius of an artist; the most heartless of landlords must have treated it with respect. The masses of plants, arranged according to their height, or in single clumps, were really a joy to the soul. This retired and solitary garden breathed comforting scents, and suggested none but sweet thoughts and graceful, nay, voluptuous pictures. On it was set that inscrutable sign-manual, which our true character stamps on everything, as soon as nothing compels us to obey the various hypocrisies, necessary as they are, which Society insists on. I looked alternately at the mass of narcissus and at the Countess, affecting to be far more in love with the flowers than with her, to carry out my part.

"'So you are very fond of flowers?' said she.

"'They are,' I replied, 'the only beings that never disappoint our cares and affection.' And I went on to deliver such a diatribe while comparing botany and the world, that we ended miles away from the dividing wall, and the Countess must have supposed me to be a wretched and wounded sufferer worthy of her pity. However, at the end of half an hour my neighbor naturally brought me back to the point; for women, when they are not in love, have all the cold blood of an experienced attorney.

"'If you insist on my leaving the paling,' said I, 'you will learn all the secrets of gardening that I want to hide; I am seeking to grow a blue dahlia, a blue rose; I am crazy for blue flowers. Is not blue the favorite color of superior souls? We are neither of us really at home; we might as well make a little door of open railings to unite our gardens.... You, too, are fond of flowers; you will see mine, I shall see yours. If you receive no visitors at all, I, for my part, have none but my uncle, the Cure of the White Friars.'

"'No,' said she, 'I will give you the right to come into my garden, my premises at any hour. Come and welcome; you will always be admitted as a neighbor with whom I hope to keep on good terms. But I like my solitude too well to burden it with any loss of independence.'

"'As you please,' said I, and with one leap I was over the paling.

"'Now, of what use would a door be?' said I, from my own domain, turning round to the Countess, and mocking her with a madman's gesture and grimace.

"For a fortnight I seemed to take no heed of my neighbor. Towards the end of May, one lovely evening, we happened both to be out on opposite sides of the paling, both walking slowly. Having reached the end, we could not help exchanging a few civil words; she found me in such deep dejection, lost in such painful meditations, that she spoke to me of hopefulness, in brief sentences that sounded like the songs with which nurses lull their babies. I then leaped the fence, and found myself for the second time at her side. The Countess led me into the house, wishing to subdue my sadness. So at last I had penetrated the sanctuary where everything was in harmony with the woman I have tried to describe to you.

"Exquisite simplicity reigned there. The interior of the little house was just such a dainty box as the art of the eighteenth century devised for the pretty profligacy of a fine gentleman. The dining-room, on the ground floor, was painted in fresco, with garlands of flowers, admirably and marvelously executed. The staircase was charmingly decorated in monochrome. The little drawing-room, opposite the dining-room, was very much faded; but the Countess had hung it with panels of tapestry of fanciful designs, taken off old screens. A bath-room came next. Upstairs there was but one bedroom, with a dressing-room, and a library which she used as her workroom. The kitchen was beneath in the basement on which the house was raised, for there was a flight of several steps outside. The balustrade of a balcony in garlands a la Pompadour concealed the roof; only the lead cornices were visible. In this retreat one was a hundred leagues from Paris.

"But for the bitter smile which occasionally played on the beautiful red lips of this pale woman, it would have been possible to believe that this violet buried in her thicket of flowers was happy. In a few days we had reached a certain degree of intimacy, the result of our close neighborhood and of the Countess' conviction that I was indifferent to women. A look would have spoilt all, and I never allowed a thought of her to be seen in my eyes. Honorine chose to regard me as an old friend. Her manner to me was the outcome of a kind of pity. Her looks, her voice, her words, all showed that she was a hundred miles away from the coquettish airs which the strictest virtue might have allowed under such circumstances. She soon gave me the right to go into the pretty workshop where she made her flowers, a retreat full of books and curiosities, as smart as a boudoir where elegance emphasized the vulgarity of the tools of her trade. The Countess had in the course of time poetized, as I may say, a thing which is at the antipodes to poetry—a manufacture.

"Perhaps of all the work a woman can do, the making of artificial flowers is that of which the details allow her to display most grace. For coloring prints she must sit bent over a table and devote herself, with some attention, to this half painting. Embroidering tapestry, as diligently as a woman must who is to earn her living by it, entails consumption or curvature of the spine. Engraving music is one of the most laborious, by the care, the minute exactitude, and the intelligence it demands. Sewing and white embroidery do not earn thirty sous a day. But the making of flowers and light articles of wear necessitates a variety of movements, gestures, ideas even, which do not take a pretty woman out of her sphere; she is still herself; she may chat, laugh, sing, or think.

"There was certainly a feeling for art in the way in which the Countess arranged on a long deal table the myriad-colored petals which were used in composing the flowers she was to produce. The saucers of color were of white china, and always clean, arranged in such order that the eye could at once see the required shade in the scale of tints. Thus the aristocratic artist saved time. A pretty little cabinet with a hundred tiny drawers, of ebony inlaid with ivory, contained the little steel moulds in which she shaped the leaves and some forms of petals. A fine Japanese bowl held the paste, which was never allowed to turn sour, and it had a fitted cover with a hinge so easy that she could lift it with a finger-tip. The wire, of iron and brass, lurked in a little drawer of the table before her.

"Under her eyes, in a Venetian glass, shaped like a flower-cup on its stem, was the living model she strove to imitate. She had a passion for achievement; she attempted the most difficult things, close racemes, the tiniest corollas, heaths, nectaries of the most variegated hues. Her hands, as swift as her thoughts, went from the table to the flower she was making, as those of an accomplished pianist fly over the keys. Her fingers seemed to be fairies, to use Perrault's expression, so infinite were the different actions of twisting, fitting, and pressure needed for the work, all hidden under grace of movement, while she adapted each motion to the result with the lucidity of instinct.

"I could not tire of admiring her as she shaped a flower from the materials sorted before her, padding the wire stem and adjusting the leaves. She displayed the genius of a painter in her bold attempts; she copied faded flowers and yellowing leaves; she struggled even with wildflowers, the most artless of all, and the most elaborate in their simplicity.

"'This art,' she would say, 'is in its infancy. If the women of Paris had a little of the genius which the slavery of the harem brings out in Oriental women, they would lend a complete language of flowers to the wreaths they wear on their head. To please my own taste as an artist I have made drooping flowers with leaves of the hue of Florentine bronze, such as are found before or after the winter. Would not such a crown on the head of a young woman whose life is a failure have a certain poetical fitness? How many things a woman might express by her head-dress! Are there not flowers for drunken Bacchantes, flowers for gloomy and stern bigots, pensive flowers for women who are bored? Botany, I believe, may be made to express every sensation and thought of the soul, even the most subtle.'

"She would employ me to stamp out the leaves, cut up material, and prepare wires for the stems. My affected desire for occupation made me soon skilful. We talked as we worked. When I had nothing to do, I read new books to her, for I had my part to keep up as a man weary of life, worn out with griefs, gloomy, sceptical, and soured. My person led to adorable banter as to

38

my purely physical resemblance—with the exception of his club foot—to Lord Byron. It was tacitly acknowledged that her own troubles, as to which she kept the most profound silence, far outweighed mine, though the causes I assigned for my misanthropy might have satisfied Young or Job.

"I will say nothing of the feelings of shame which tormented me as I inflicted on my heart, like the beggars in the street, false wounds to excite the compassion of that enchanting woman. I soon appreciated the extent of my devotedness by learning to estimate the baseness of a spy. The expressions of sympathy bestowed on me would have comforted the greatest grief. This charming creature, weaned from the world, and for so many years alone, having, besides love, treasures of kindliness to bestow, offered these to me with childlike effusiveness and such compassion as would inevitably have filled with bitterness any profligate who should have fallen in love with her; for, alas, it was all charity, all sheer pity. Her renunciation of love, her dread of what is called happiness for women, she proclaimed with equal vehemence and candor. These happy days proved to me that a woman's friendship is far superior to her love.

"I suffered the revelations of my sorrows to be dragged from me with as many grimaces as a young lady allows herself before sitting down to the piano, so conscious are they of the annoyance that will follow. As you may imagine, the necessity for overcoming my dislike to speak had induced the Countess to strengthen the bonds of our intimacy; but she found in me so exact a counterpart of her own antipathy to love, that I fancied she was well content with the chance which had brought to her desert island a sort of Man Friday. Solitude was perhaps beginning to weigh on her. At the same time, there was nothing of the coquette in her; nothing survived of the woman; she did not feel that she had a heart, she told me, excepting in the ideal world where she found refuge. I involuntarily compared these two lives—hers and the Count's:—his, all activity, agitation, and emotion; hers, all inaction, quiescence, and stagnation. The woman and the man were admirably obedient to their nature. My misanthropy allowed me to utter cynical sallies against men and women both, and I indulged in them, hoping to bring Honorine to the confidential point; but she was not to be caught in any trap, and I began to understand that mulish obstinacy which is commoner among women than is generally supposed.

"'The Orientals are right,' I said to her one evening, 'when they shut you up and regard you merely as the playthings of their pleasure. Europe has been well punished for having admitted you to form an element of society and for accepting you on an equal footing. In my opinion, woman is the most dishonorable and cowardly being to be found. Nay, and that is where her charm lies. Where would be the pleasure of hunting a tame thing? When once a woman has inspired a man's passion, she is to him for ever sacred; in his eyes she is hedged round by an imprescriptible prerogative. In men gratitude for past delights is eternal. Though he should find his mistress grown old or unworthy, the woman still has rights over his heart; but to you women the man you have loved is as nothing to you; nay, more, he is unpardonable in one thing—he lives on! You dare not own it, but you all have in your hearts the feeling which that popular calumny called tradition ascribes to the Lady of the Tour de Nesle: "What a pity it is that we cannot live on love as we live on fruit, and that when we have had our fill, nothing should survive but the remembrance of pleasure!"'

"'God has, no doubt, reserved such perfect bliss for Paradise,' said she. 'But,' she added, 'if your argument seems to you very witty, to me it has the disadvantage of being false. What can those women be who give themselves up to a succession of loves?' she asked, looking at me as the Virgin in Ingres' picture looks at Louis XIII. offering her his kingdom.

"'You are an actress in good faith,' said I, 'for you gave me a look just now which would make the fame of an actress. Still, lovely as you are, you have loved; *ergo*, you forget.'

"'I!' she exclaimed, evading my question, 'I am not a woman. I am a nun, and seventy-two years old!'

"'Then, how can you so positively assert that you feel more keenly than I? Sorrow has but one form for women. The only misfortunes they regard are disappointments of the heart.'

"She looked at me sweetly, and, like all women when stuck between the issues of a dilemma, or held in the clutches of truth, she persisted, nevertheless, in her wilfulness.

"'I am a nun,' she said, 'and you talk to me of the world where I shall never again set foot.'

"'Not even in thought?' said I.

"'Is the world so much to be desired?' she replied. 'Oh! when my mind wanders, it goes higher. The angel of perfection, the beautiful angel Gabriel, often sings in my heart. If I were rich, I should work, all the same, to keep me from soaring too often on the many-tinted wings of the angel, and wandering in the world of fancy. There are meditations which are the ruin of us women! I owe much peace of mind to my flowers, though sometimes they fail to occupy me. On some days I find my soul invaded by a purposeless expectancy; I cannot banish some idea which takes possession of me, which seems to make my fingers clumsy. I feel that some great event is impending, that my life is about to change; I listen vaguely, I stare into the darkness, I have no liking for my work, and after a thousand fatigues I find life once more—everyday life. Is this a warning from heaven? I ask myself——'

"After three months of this struggle between two diplomates, concealed under the semblance of youthful melancholy, and a woman whose disgust of life made her invulnerable, I told the Count that it was impossible to drag this tortoise out of her shell; it must be broken. The evening before, in our last quite friendly discussion, the Countess had exclaimed:

"'Lucretia's dagger wrote in letters of blood the watchword of woman's charter: *Liberty!*'

"From that moment the Count left me free to act.

"'I have been paid a hundred francs for the flowers and caps I made this week!' Honorine exclaimed gleefully one Saturday evening when I went to visit her in the little sitting-room on the ground floor, which the unavowed proprietor had had regilt.

"It was ten o'clock. The twilight of July and a glorious moon lent us their misty light. Gusts of mingled perfumes soothed the soul; the Countess was clinking in her hand the five gold pieces given to her by a supposititious dealer in fashionable frippery, another of Octave's accomplices found for him by a judge, M. Popinot.

"'I earn my living by amusing myself,' said she; 'I am free, when men, armed with their laws, have tried to make us slaves. Oh, I have transports of pride every Saturday! In short, I like M. Gaudissart's gold pieces as much as Lord Byron, your double, liked Mr. Murray's.'

"'This is not becoming in a woman,' said I.

"'Pooh! Am I a woman? I am a boy gifted with a soft soul, that is all; a boy whom no woman can torture——'

"'Your life is the negation of your whole being,' I replied. 'What? You, on whom God has lavished His choicest treasures of love and beauty, do you never wish——'

"'For what?' said she, somewhat disturbed by a speech which, for the first time, gave the lie to the part I had assumed.

"'For a pretty little child, with curling hair, running, playing among the flowers, like a flower itself of life and love, and calling you mother!'

"I waited for an answer. A too prolonged silence led me to perceive the terrible effect of my words, though the darkness at first concealed it. Leaning on her sofa, the Countess had not indeed fainted, but frozen under a nervous attack of which the first chill, as gentle as everything that was part of her, felt, as she afterwards said, like the influence of a most insidious poison. I called Madame Gobain, who came and led away her mistress, laid her on her bed, unlaced her, undressed her, and restored her, not to life, it is true, but to the consciousness of some dreadful suffering. I meanwhile walked up and down the path behind the house, weeping, and doubting my success. I only wished to give up this part of the bird-catcher which I had so rashly assumed. Madame Gobain, who came down and found me with my face wet with tears, hastily went up again to say to the Countess:

"'What has happened, madame? Monsieur Maurice is crying like a child.'

"Roused to action by the evil interpretation that might be put on our mutual behavior, she summoned superhuman strength to put on a wrapper and come down to me.

"'You are not the cause of this attack,' said she. 'I am subject to these spasms, a sort of cramp of the heart——'

"'And will you not tell me of your troubles?' said I, in a voice which cannot be affected, as I wiped away my tears. 'Have you not just now told me that you have been a mother, and have been so unhappy as to lose your child?'

"'Marie!' she called as she rang the bell. Gobain came in.

"'Bring lights and some tea,' said she, with the calm decision of a Mylady clothed in the armor of pride by the dreadful English training which you know too well.

"When the housekeeper had lighted the tapers and closed the shutters, the Countess showed me a mute countenance; her indomitable pride and gravity, worthy of a savage, had already reasserted their mastery. She said:

"'Do you know why I like Lord Byron so much? It is because he suffered as animals do. Of what use are complaints when they are not an elegy like Manfred's, nor bitter mockery like Don Juan's, nor a reverie like Childe Harold's? Nothing shall be known of me. My heart is a poem that I lay before God.'

"'If I chose——' said I.

"'If?' she repeated.

"'I have no interest in anything,' I replied, 'so I cannot be inquisitive; but, if I chose, I could know all your secrets by to-morrow.'

"'I defy you!' she exclaimed, with ill-disguised uneasiness.

"'Seriously?'

"'Certainly,' said she, tossing her head. 'If such a crime is possible, I ought to know it.'

"'In the first place, madame,' I went on, pointing to her hands, 'those pretty fingers, which are enough to show that you are not a mere girl—were they made for toil? Then you call yourself Madame Gobain, you, who, in my presence the other day on receiving a letter, said to Marie: "Here, this is for you?" Marie is the real Madame Gobain; so you conceal your name behind that of your housekeeper.—Fear nothing, madame, from me. You have in me the most devoted friend you will ever have: Friend, do you understand me? I give this word its sacred and pathetic meaning, so profaned in France, where we apply it to our enemies. And your friend, who will defend you against everything, only wishes that you should be as happy as such a woman ought to be. Who can tell whether the pain I have involuntarily caused you was not a voluntary act?'

"'Yes,' replied she with threatening audacity, 'I insist on it. Be curious, and tell me all that you can find out about me; but,' and she held up her finger, 'you must also tell me by what means you obtain your information. The preservation of the small happiness I enjoy here depends on the steps you take.'

"'That means that you will fly——'

"'On wings!' she cried, 'to the New World——'

"'Where you will be at the mercy of the brutal passions you will inspire,' said I, interrupting her. 'Is it not the very essence of genius and beauty to shine, to attract men's gaze, to excite desires and evil thoughts? Paris is a desert with Bedouins; Paris is the only place in the world where those who must work for their livelihood can hide their life. What have you to complain of? Who am I? An additional servant—M. Gobain, that is all. If you have to fight a duel, you may need a second.'

"'Never mind; find out who I am. I have already said that I insist. Now, I beg that you will,' she went on, with the grace which you ladies have at command," said the Consul, looking at the ladies.

"'Well, then, to-morrow, at the same hour, I will tell you what I may have discovered,' replied I. 'But do not therefore hate me! Will you behave like other women?'

"'What do other women do?'

"'They lay upon us immense sacrifices, and when we have made them, they reproach us for it some time later as if it were an injury.'

"'They are right if the thing required appears to be a sacrifice!' replied she pointedly.

"'Instead of sacrifices, say efforts and——'

"'It would be an impertinence,' said she.

"'Forgive me,' said I. 'I forget that woman and the Pope are infallible.'

"'Good heavens!' said she after a long pause, 'only two words would be enough to destroy the peace so dearly bought, and which I enjoy like a fraud ——'

"She rose and paid no further heed to me.

"'Where can I go?' she said. 'What is to become of me?—Must I leave this quiet retreat, that I had arranged with such care to end my days in?'

"'To end your days!' exclaimed I with visible alarm. 'Has it never struck you that a time would come when you could no longer work, when competition will lower the price of flowers and articles of fashion——?'

"'I have already saved a thousand crowns,' she said.

"'Heavens! what privations such a sum must represent!' I exclaimed.

"'Leave me,' said she, 'till to-morrow. This evening I am not myself; I must be alone. Must I not save my strength in case of disaster? For, if you should learn anything, others besides you would be informed, and then—Good-night,' she added shortly, dismissing me with an imperious gesture.

"'The battle is to-morrow, then,' I replied with a smile, to keep up the appearance of indifference I had given to the scene. But as I went down the avenue I repeated the words:

"'The battle is to-morrow.'

"Octave's anxiety was equal to Honorine's. The Count and I remained together till two in the morning, walking to and fro by the trenches of the Bastille, like two generals who, on the eve of a battle, calculate all the chances, examine the ground, and perceive that the victory must depend on an opportunity to be seized half-way through the fight. These two divided beings would each lie awake, one in the hope, the other in agonizing dread of reunion. The real dramas of life are not in circumstances, but in feelings; they are played in the heart, or, if you please, in that vast realm which we ought to call the Spiritual World. Octave and Honorine moved and lived altogether in the world of lofty spirits.

"I was punctual. At ten next evening I was, for the first time, shown into a charming bedroom furnished with white and blue—the nest of this wounded dove. The Countess looked at me, and was about to speak, but was stricken dumb by my respectful demeanor.

"'Madame la Comtesse,' said I with a grave smile.

"The poor woman, who had risen, dropped back into her chair and remained there, sunk in an attitude of grief, which I should have liked to see perpetuated by a great painter.

"'You are,' I went on, 'the wife of the noblest and most highly respected of men; of a man who is acknowledged to be great, but who is far greater in his conduct to you than he is in the eyes of the world. You and he are two lofty natures.—Where do you suppose yourself to be living?' I asked her.

"'In my own house,' she replied, opening her eyes with a wide stare of astonishment.

"'In Count Octave's,' I replied. 'You have been tricked. M. Lenormand, the usher of the Court, is not the real owner; he is only a screen for your husband. The delightful seclusion you enjoy is the Count's work, the money you earn is paid by him, and his protection extends to the most trivial details of your existence. Your husband has saved you in the eyes of the world; he has assigned plausible reasons for your disappearance; he professes to hope that you were not lost in the wreck of the *Cecile*, the ship in which you sailed for Havana to secure the fortune to be left to you by an old aunt, who might have forgotten you; you embarked, escorted by two ladies of her family and an old man-servant. The Count says that he has sent agents to various spots, and received letters which give him great hopes. He takes as many precautions to hide you from all eyes as you take yourself. In short, he obeys you...'

"'That is enough,' she said. 'I want to know but one thing more. From whom have you obtained all these details?'

"'Well, madame, my uncle got a place for a penniless youth as secretary to the Commissary of police in this part of Paris. That young man told me everything. If you leave this house this evening, however stealthily, your husband will know where you are gone, and his care will follow you everywhere.—How could a woman so clever as you are believe that shopkeepers buy flowers and caps as dear as they sell them? Ask a thousand crowns for a bouquet, and you will get it. No mother's tenderness was ever more ingenious than your husband's! I have learned from the porter of this house that the Count often comes behind the fence when all are asleep, to see the glimmer of your nightlight! Your large cashmere shawl cost six thousand francs—your old-clothes-seller brings you, as second hand, things fresh from the best makers. In short, you are living here like Venus in the toils of Vulcan; but you are alone in your prison by the devices of a sublime magnanimity, sublime for seven years past, and at every hour.'

"The Countess was trembling as a trapped swallow trembles while, as you hold it in your hand, it strains its neck to look about it with wild eyes. She shook with a nervous spasm, studying me with a defiant look. Her dry eyes glittered with a light that was almost hot: still, she was a woman! The moment came when her tears forced their way, and she wept—not because she was touched, but because she was helpless; they were tears of desperation. She had believed herself independent and free; marriage weighed on her as the prison cell does on the captive.

"'I will go!' she cried through her tears. 'He forces me to it; I will go where no one certainly will come after me.'

"'What,' I said, 'you would kill yourself?—Madame, you must have some very powerful reasons for not wishing to return to Comte Octave.'

"'Certainly I have!'

"'Well, then, tell them to me; tell them to my uncle. In us you will find two devoted advisers. Though in the confessional my uncle is a priest, he never is one in a drawing-room. We will hear you; we will try to find a solution of the problems you may lay before us; and if you are the dupe or the victim of some misapprehension, perhaps we can clear the matter up. Your soul, I believe, is pure; but if you have done wrong, your fault is fully expiated.... At any rate, remember that in me you have a most sincere friend. If you should wish to evade the Count's tyranny, I will find you the means; he shall never find you.'

"'Oh! there is always a convent!' said she.

"'Yes. But the Count, as Minister of State, can procure your rejection by every convent in the world. Even though he is powerful, I will save you from him—; but—only when you have demonstrated to me that you cannot and ought not to return to him. Oh! do not fear that you would escape his power only to fall into mine,' I added, noticing a glance of horrible suspicion, full of exaggerated dignity. 'You shall have peace, solitude, and independence; in short, you shall be as free and as little annoyed as if you were an ugly, cross old maid. I myself would never be able to see you without your consent.'

"'And how? By what means?'

"'That is my secret. I am not deceiving you, of that you may be sure. Prove to me that this is the only life you can lead, that it is preferable to that of the Comtesse Octave, rich, admired, in one of the finest houses in Paris, beloved by her husband, a happy mother... and I will decide in your favor.'

"'But,' said she, 'will there never be a man who understands me?'

"'No. And that is why I appeal to religion to decide between us. The Cure of the White Friars is a saint, seventy-five years of age. My uncle is not a Grand Inquisitor, he is Saint John; but for you he will be Fenelon—the Fenelon who said to the Duc de Bourgogne: 'Eat a calf on a Friday by all means, monseigneur. But be a Christian.'

"'Nay, nay, monsieur, the convent is my last hope and my only refuge. There is none but God who can understand me. No man, not Saint Augustine himself, the tenderest of the Fathers of the Church, could enter into the scruples of my conscience, which are to me as the circles of Dante's hell, whence there is no escape. Another than my husband, a different man, however unworthy of the offering, has had all my love. No, he has not had it, for he did not take it; I gave it him as a mother gives her child a wonderful toy, which it breaks. For me there never could be two loves. In some natures love can never be on trial; it is, or it is not. When it comes, when it rises up, it is complete.—Well, that life of eighteen months was to me a life of eighteen years; I threw into it all the faculties of my being, which were not impoverished by their effusiveness; they were exhausted by that delusive intimacy in which I alone was genuine. For me the cup of happiness is not drained, nor empty; and nothing can refill it, for it is broken. I am out of the fray; I have no weapons left. Having thus utterly abandoned myself, what am I?—the leavings of a feast. I had but one name bestowed on me, Honorine, as I had but one heart. My husband had the young girl, a worthless lover had the woman—there is nothing left!—Then let myself be loved! that is the great idea you mean to utter to me. Oh! but I still am something, and I rebel at the idea of being a prostitute! Yes, by the light of the conflagration I saw clearly; and I tell you—well, I could imagine surrendering to another man's love, but to Octave's?—No, never.'

"'Ah! you love him,' I said.

"'I esteem him, respect him, venerate him; he never has done me the smallest hurt; he is kind, he is tender; but I can never more love him. However,' she went on, 'let us talk no more of this. Discussion makes everything small. I will express my notions on this subject in writing to you, for at this moment they are suffocating me; I am feverish, my feet are standing in the ashes of my Paraclete. All that I see, these things which I believed I had earned by my labor, now remind me of everything I wish to forget. Ah! I must fly from hence as I fled from my home.'

"'Where will you go?' I asked. 'Can a woman exist unprotected? At thirty, in all the glory of your beauty, rich in powers of which you have no suspicion, full of tenderness to be bestowed, are you prepared to live in the wilderness where I could hide you?—Be quite easy. The Count, who for nine years has never allowed himself to be seen here, will never go there without your permission. You have his sublime devotion of nine years as a guarantee for your tranquillity. You may therefore discuss the future in perfect confidence with my uncle and me. My uncle has as much influence as a Minister of State. So compose yourself; do not exaggerate your misfortune. A priest whose hair has grown white in the exercise of his functions is not a boy; you will be understood by him to whom every passion has been confided for nearly fifty years now, and who weighs in his hands the ponderous heart of kings and princes. If he is stern under his stole, in the presence of your flowers he will be as tender as they are, and as indulgent as his Divine Master.'

"I left the Countess at midnight; she was apparently calm, but depressed, and had some secret purpose which no perspicacity could guess. I found the Count a few paces off, in the Rue Saint-Maur. Drawn by an irresistible attraction, he had quitted the spot on the Boulevards where we had agreed to meet.

"'What a night my poor child will go through!' he exclaimed, when I had finished my account of the scene that had just taken place. 'Supposing I were to go to her!' he added; 'supposing she were to see me suddenly?'

"'At this moment she is capable of throwing herself out of the window,' I replied. 'The Countess is one of those Lucretias who could not survive any violence, even if it were done by a man into whose arms she could throw herself.'

"'You are young,' he answered; 'you do not know that in a soul tossed by such dreadful alternatives the will is like waters of a lake lashed by a tempest; the wind changes every instant, and the waves are driven now to one shore, now to the other. During this night the chances are quite as great that on seeing me Honorine might rush into my arms as that she would throw herself out of the window.'

"'And you would accept the equal chances,' said I.

"'Well, come,' said he, 'I have at home, to enable me to wait till to-morrow, a dose of opium which Desplein prepared for me to send me to sleep without any risk!'

"Next day at noon Gobain brought me a letter, telling me that the Countess had gone to bed at six, worn out with fatigue, and that, having taken a soothing draught prepared by the chemist, she had now fallen asleep.

"This is her letter, of which I kept a copy—for you, mademoiselle," said the Consul, addressing Camille, "know all the resources of art, the tricks of style, and the efforts made in their compositions by writers who do not lack skill; but you will acknowledge that literature could never find such language in its assumed pathos; there is nothing so terrible as truth. Here is the letter written by this woman, or rather by this anguish:—

"'MONSIEUR MAURICE,—

"'I know all your uncle would say to me; he is not better informed than my own conscience. Conscience is the interpreter of God to man. I know that if I am not reconciled to Octave, I shall be damned; that is the sentence of religious law. Civil law condemns me to obey, cost what it may. If my husband does not reject me, the world will regard me as pure, as virtuous, whatever I may have done. Yes, that much is sublime in marriage; society ratifies the husband's forgiveness; but it forgets that the forgiveness must be accepted. Legally, religiously, and from the world's point of view I ought to go back to Octave. Keeping only to the human aspect of the question, is it not cruel to refuse him happiness, to deprive him of children, to wipe his name out of the Golden Book and the list of peers? My sufferings, my repugnance, my feelings, all my egoism—for I know that I am an egoist—ought to be sacrificed to the family. I shall be a mother; the caresses of my child will wipe away many tears! I shall be very happy; I certainly shall be much looked up to. I shall ride, haughty and wealthy, in a handsome carriage! I shall have servants and a fine house, and be the queen of as many parties as there are weeks in the year. The world will receive me handsomely. I shall not have to climb up again to the heaven of aristocracy, I shall never have come down from it. So God, the law, society are all in accord.

"'"What are you rebelling against?" I am asked from the height of heaven, from the pulpit, from the judge's bench, and from the throne, whose august intervention may at need be invoked by the Count. Your uncle, indeed, at need, would speak to me of a certain celestial grace which will flood my heart when I know the pleasure of doing my duty.

"'God, the law, the world, and Octave all wish me to live, no doubt. Well, if there is no other difficulty, my reply cuts the knot: I will not live. I will become white and innocent again; for I will lie in my shroud, white with the blameless pallor of death. This is not in the least "mulish obstinacy." That mulish obstinacy of which you jestingly accused me is in a woman the result of confidence, of a vision of the future. Though my husband, sublimely generous, may forget all, I shall not forget. Does forgetfulness depend on our will? When a widow re-marries, love makes a girl of her; she marries a man

49

she loves. But I cannot love the Count. It all lies in that, do not you see?

"'Every time my eyes met his I should see my sin in them, even when his were full of love. The greatness of his generosity would be the measure of the greatness of my crime. My eyes, always uneasy, would be for ever reading an invisible condemnation. My heart would be full of confused and struggling memories; marriage can never move me to the cruel rapture, the mortal delirium of passion. I should kill my husband by my coldness, by comparisons which he would guess, though hidden in the depths of my conscience. Oh! on the day when I should read a trace of involuntary, even of suppressed reproach in a furrow on his brow, in a saddened look, in some imperceptible gesture, nothing could hold me: I should be lying with a fractured skull on the pavement, and find that less hard than my husband. It might be my own over-susceptibility that would lead me to this horrible but welcome death; I might die the victim of an impatient mood in Octave caused by some matter of business, or be deceived by some unjust suspicion. Alas! I might even mistake some proof of love for a sign of contempt!

"'What torture on both sides! Octave would be always doubting me, I doubting him. I, quite involuntarily, should give him a rival wholly unworthy of him, a man whom I despise, but with whom I have known raptures branded on me with fire, which are my shame, but which I cannot forget.

"'Have I shown you enough of my heart? No one, monsieur, can convince me that love may be renewed, for I neither can nor will accept love from any one. A young bride is like a plucked flower; but a guilty wife is like a flower that had been walked over. You, who are a florist, you know whether it is ever possible to restore the broken stem, to revive the faded colors, to make the sap flow again in the tender vessels of which the whole vegetative function lies in their perfect rigidity. If some botanist should attempt the operation, could his genius smooth out the folds of the bruised corolla? If he could remake a flower, he would be God! God alone can remake me! I am drinking the bitter cup of expiation; but as I drink it I painfully spell out this sentence: Expiation is not annihilation.

"'In my little house, alone, I eat my bread soaked in tears; but no one sees me eat nor sees me weep. If I go back to Octave, I must give up my tears—they would offend him. Oh! monsieur, how many virtues must a woman tread under foot, not to give herself, but to restore herself to a betrayed husband? Who could count them? God alone; for He alone can know and encourage the horrible refinements at which the angels must turn pale. Nay, I will go further. A woman has courage in the presence of her husband if he knows nothing; she shows a sort of fierce strength in her hypocrisy; she deceives him to secure him double happiness. But common knowledge is surely degrading.

Supposing I could exchange humiliation for ecstasy? Would not Octave at last feel that my consent was sheer depravity? Marriage is based on esteem, on sacrifices on both sides; but neither Octave nor I could esteem each other the day after our reunion. He would have disgraced me by a love like that of an old man for a courtesan, and I should for ever feel the shame of being a chattel instead of a lady. I should represent pleasure, and not virtue, in his house. These are the bitter fruits of such a sin. I have made myself a bed where I can only toss on burning coals, a sleepless pillow.

"'Here, when I suffer, I bless my sufferings; I say to God, "I thank Thee!" But in my husband's house I should be full of terror, tasting joys to which I have no right.

"'All this, monsieur, is not argument; it is the feeling of a soul made vast and hollow by seven years of suffering. Finally, must I make a horrible confession? I shall always feel at my bosom the lips of a child conceived in rapture and joy, and in the belief in happiness, of a child I nursed for seven months, that I shall bear in my womb all the days of my life. If other children should draw their nourishment from me, they would drink in tears mingling with the milk, and turning it sour. I seem a light thing, you regard me as a child—Ah yes! I have a child's memory, the memory which returns to us on the verge of the tomb. So, you see, there is not a situation in that beautiful life to which the world and my husband's love want to recall me, which is not a false position, which does not cover a snare or reveal a precipice down which I must fall, torn by pitiless rocks. For five years now I have been wandering in the sandy desert of the future without finding a place convenient to repent in, because my soul is possessed by true repentance.

"'Religion has its answers ready to all this, and I know them by heart. This suffering, these difficulties, are my punishment, she says, and God will give me strength to endure them. This, monsieur, is an argument to certain pious souls gifted with an energy which I have not. I have made my choice between this hell, where God does not forbid my blessing Him, and the hell that awaits me under Count Octave's roof.

"'One word more. If I were still a girl, with the experience I now have, my husband is the man I should choose; but that is the very reason of my refusal. I could not bear to blush before that man. What! I should be always on my knees, he always standing upright; and if we were to exchange positions, I should scorn him! I will not be better treated by him in consequence of my sin. The angel who might venture under such circumstances on certain liberties which are permissible when both are equally blameless, is not on earth; he dwells in heaven! Octave is full of delicate feeling, I know; but even in his soul (which, however generous, is a man's soul after all) there is no guarantee for the new life I should lead with him.

"'Come then, and tell me where I may find the solitude, the peace, the silence, so kindly to irreparable woes, which you promised me.'

"After making this copy of the letter to preserve it complete, I went to the Rue Payenne. Anxiety had conquered the power of opium. Octave was walking up and down his garden like a madman.

"'Answer that!' said I, giving him his wife's letter. 'Try to reassure the modesty of experience. It is rather more difficult than conquering the modesty of ignorance, which curiosity helps to betray.'

"'She is mine!' cried the Count, whose face expressed joy as he went on reading the letter.

"He signed to me with his hand to leave him to himself. I understood that extreme happiness and extreme pain obey the same laws; I went in to receive Madame de Courteville and Amelie, who were to dine with the Count that day. However handsome Mademoiselle de Courteville might be, I felt, on seeing her once more, that love has three aspects, and that the women who can inspire us with perfect love are very rare. As I involuntarily compared Amelie with Honorine, I found the erring wife more attractive than the pure girl. To Honorine's heart fidelity had not been a duty, but the inevitable; while Amelie would serenely pronounce the most solemn promises without knowing their purport or to what they bound her. The crushed, the dead woman, so to speak, the sinner to be reinstated, seemed to me sublime; she incited the special generosities of a man's nature; she demanded all the treasures of the heart, all the resources of strength; she filled his life and gave the zest of a conflict to happiness; whereas Amelie, chaste and confiding, would settle down into the sphere of peaceful motherhood, where the commonplace must be its poetry, and where my mind would find no struggle and no victory.

"Of the plains of Champagne and the snowy, storm-beaten but sublime Alps, what young man would choose the chalky, monotonous level? No; such comparisons are fatal and wrong on the threshold of the Mairie. Alas! only the experience of life can teach us that marriage excludes passion, that a family cannot have its foundation on the tempests of love. After having dreamed of impossible love, with its infinite caprices, after having tasted the tormenting delights of the ideal, I saw before me modest reality. Pity me, for what could be expected! At five-and-twenty I did not trust myself; but I took a manful resolution.

"I went back to the Count to announce the arrival of his relations, and I saw him grown young again in the reflected light of hope.

"'What ails you, Maurice?' said he, struck by my changed expression.

"'Monsieur le Comte——'

"'No longer Octave? You, to whom I shall owe my life, my happiness——'

"'My dear Octave, if you should succeed in bringing the Countess back to her duty, I have studied her well'—(he looked at me as Othello must have looked at Iago when Iago first contrived to insinuate a suspicion into the Moor's mind)—'she must never see me again; she must never know that Maurice was your secretary. Never mention my name to her, or all will be undone…. You have got me an appointment as Maitre des Requetes—well, get me instead some diplomatic post abroad, a consulship, and do not think of my marrying Amelie.—Oh! do not be uneasy,' I added, seeing him draw himself up, 'I will play my part to the end.'

"'Poor boy!' said he, taking my hand, which he pressed, while he kept back the tears that were starting to his eyes.

"'You gave me the gloves,' I said, laughing, 'but I have not put them on; that is all.'

"We then agreed as to what I was to do that evening at Honorine's house, whither I presently returned. It was now August; the day had been hot and stormy, but the storm hung overhead, the sky was like copper; the scent of the flowers was heavy, I felt as if I were in an oven, and caught myself wishing that the Countess might have set out for the Indies; but she was sitting on a wooden bench shaped like a sofa, under an arbor, in a loose dress of white muslin fastened with blue bows, her hair unadorned in waving bands over her cheeks, her feet on a small wooden stool, and showing a little way beyond her skirt. She did not rise; she showed me with her hand to the seat by her side, saying:

"'Now, is not life at a deadlock for me?'

"'Life as you have made it, I replied. 'But not the life I propose to make for you; for, if you choose, you may be very happy….'

"'How?' said she; her whole person was a question.

"'Your letter is in the Count's hands.'

"Honorine started like a frightened doe, sprang to a few paces off, walked down the garden, turned about, remained standing for some minutes, and finally went in to sit alone in the drawing-room, where I joined her, after giving her time to get accustomed to the pain of this poniard thrust.

"'You—a friend? Say rather a traitor! A spy, perhaps, sent by my husband.'

"Instinct in women is as strong as the perspicacity of great men.

"'You wanted an answer to your letter, did you not? And there was but one man in the world who could write it. You must read the reply, my dear Countess; and if after reading it you still find that your life is a deadlock, the spy will prove himself a friend; I will place you in a convent whence the Count's power cannot drag you. But, before going there, let us consider the other side of the question. There is a law, alike divine and human, which even hatred affects to obey, and which commands us not to condemn the accused without hearing his defence. Till now you have passed condemnation, as children do, with your ears stopped. The devotion of seven years has its claims. So you must read the answer your husband will send you. I have forwarded to him, through my uncle, a copy of your letter, and my uncle asked him what his reply would be if his wife wrote him a letter in such terms. Thus you are not compromised. He will himself bring the Count's answer. In the presence of that saintly man, and in mine, out of respect for your own dignity, you must read it, or you will be no better than a wilful, passionate child. You must make this sacrifice to the world, to the law, and to God.'

"As she saw in this concession no attack on her womanly resolve, she consented. All the labor or four or five months had been building up to this moment. But do not the Pyramids end in a point on which a bird may perch? The Count had set all his hopes on this supreme instant, and he had reached it.

"In all my life I remember nothing more formidable than my uncle's entrance into that little Pompadour drawing-room, at ten that evening. The fine head, with its silver hair thrown into relief by the entirely black dress, and the divinely calm face, had a magical effect on the Comtesse Honorine; she had the feeling of cool balm on her wounds, and beamed in the reflection of that virtue which gave light without knowing it.

"'Monsieur the Cure of the White Friars,' said old Gobain.

"'Are you come, uncle, with a message of happiness and peace?' said I.

"'Happiness and peace are always to be found in obedience to the precepts of the Church,' replied my uncle, and he handed the Countess the following letter:—

"'MY DEAR HONORINE,—

"'If you had but done me the favor of trusting me, if you had read the letter I wrote to you five years since, you would have spared yourself five years of useless labor, and of privations which have grieved me deeply. In it I proposed an arrangement of which the stipulations will relieve all your fears, and make our domestic life possible. I have much to reproach myself with, and in seven years of sorrow I have discovered all my errors. I misunderstood marriage. I failed to scent danger when it threatened you. An angel was in the house. The Lord bid me guard it well! The Lord has punished me for my audacious confidence.

"'You cannot give yourself a single lash without striking me. Have mercy on me, my dear Honorine. I so fully appreciated your susceptibilities that I would not bring you back to the old house in the Rue Payenne, where I can live without you, but which I could not bear to see again with you. I am decorating, with great pleasure, another house, in the Faubourg Saint-Honore, to which, in hope, I conduct not a wife whom I owe to her ignorance of life, and secured to me by law, but a sister who will allow me to press on her brow such a kiss as a father gives the daughter he blesses every day.

"'Will you bereave me of the right I have conquered from your despair— that of watching more closely over your needs, your pleasures, your life even? Women have one heart always on their side, always abounding in excuses— their mother's; you never knew any mother but my mother, who would have brought you back to me. But how is it that you never guessed that I had for you the heart of a mother, both of my mother and of your own? Yes, dear, my affection is neither mean nor grasping; it is one of those which will never let any annoyance last long enough to pucker the brow of the child it worships. What can you think of the companion of your childhood, Honorine, if you believe him capable of accepting kisses given in trembling, of living between delight and anxiety? Do not fear that you will be exposed to the laments of a suppliant passion; I would not want you back until I felt certain of my own strength to leave you in perfect freedom.

"'Your solitary pride has exaggerated the difficulties. You may, if you will, look on at the life of a brother, or of a father, without either suffering or joy; but you will find neither mockery nor indifference, nor have any doubt as to his intentions. The warmth of the atmosphere in which you live will be always equable and genial, without tempests, without a possible squall. If, later, when you feel secure that you are as much at home as in your own little house, you desire to try some other elements of happiness, pleasures, or amusements, you can expand their circle at your will. The tenderness of a mother knows neither contempt nor pity. What is it? Love without desire. Well, in me admiration shall hide every sentiment in which you might see an offence.

"'Thus, living side by side, we may both be magnanimous. In you the kindness of a sister, the affectionate thoughtfulness of a friend, will satisfy the ambition of him who wishes to be your life's companion; and you may measure his tenderness by the care he will take to conceal it. Neither you nor I will be jealous of the past, for we may each acknowledge that the other has sense enough to look only straight forward.

"'Thus you will be at home in your new house exactly as you are in the Rue Saint-Maur; unapproachable, alone, occupied as you please, living by your own law; but having in addition the legitimate protection, of which you are now exacting the most chivalrous labors of love, with the consideration which lends so much lustre to a woman, and the fortune which will allow of your doing many good works. Honorine, when you long for an unnecessary absolution, you have only to ask for it; it will not be forced upon you by the Church or by the Law; it will wait on your pride, on your own impulsion. My wife might indeed have to fear all the things you dread; but not my friend and sister, towards whom I am bound to show every form and refinement of politeness. To see you happy is enough happiness for me; I have proved this for the seven years past. The guarantee for this, Honorine, is to be seen in all the flowers made by you, carefully preserved, and watered by my tears. Like the *quipos*, the tally cords of the Peruvians, they are the record of our sorrows.

"'If this secret compact does not suit you, my child, I have begged the saintly man who takes charge of this letter not to say a word in my behalf. I will not owe your return to the terrors threatened by the Church, nor to the bidding of the Law. I will not accept the simple and quiet happiness that I ask from any one but yourself. If you persist in condemning me to the lonely life, bereft even of a fraternal smile, which I have led for nine years, if you remain in your solitude and show no sign, my will yields to yours. Understand me perfectly: you shall be no more troubled than you have been until this day. I will get rid of the crazy fellow who has meddled in your concerns, and has perhaps caused you some annoyance...'

"'Monsieur,' said Honorine, folding up the letter, which she placed in her bosom, and looking at my uncle, 'thank you very much. I will avail myself of Monsieur le Comte's permission to remain here——'

"'Ah!' I exclaimed.

"This exclamation made my uncle look at me uneasily, and won from the Countess a mischievous glance, which enlightened me as to her motives.

"Honorine had wanted to ascertain whether I were an actor, a bird snarer; and I had the melancholy satisfaction of deceiving her by my exclamation, which was one of those cries from the heart which women understand so well.

"'Ah, Maurice,' said she, 'you know how to love.'

"The light that flashed in my eyes was another reply which would have dissipated the Countess' uneasiness if she still had any. Thus the Count found me useful to the very last.

"Honorine then took out the Count's letter again to finish reading it. My uncle signed to me, and I rose.

"'Let us leave the Countess,' said he.

"'You are going already Maurice?' she said, without looking at me.

"She rose, and still reading, followed us to the door. On the threshold she took my hand, pressed it very affectionately, and said, 'We shall meet again...'

"'No,' I replied, wringing her hand, so that she cried out. 'You love your husband. I leave to-morrow.'

"And I rushed away, leaving my uncle, to whom she said:

"'Why, what is the matter with your nephew?'

"The good Abbe completed my work by pointing to his head and heart, as much as to say, 'He is mad, madame; you must forgive him!' and with all the more truth, because he really thought it.

"Six days after, I set out with an appointment as vice-consul in Spain, in a large commercial town, where I could quickly qualify to rise in the career of a consul, to which I now restricted my ambition. After I had established myself there, I received this letter from the Count:—

"'MY DEAR MAURICE,—

"'If I were happy, I should not write to you, but I have entered on a new life of suffering. I have grown young again in my desires, with all the impatience of a man of forty, and the prudence of a diplomatist, who has learned to moderate his passion. When you left I had not yet been admitted to the *pavillon* in the Rue Saint-Maur, but a letter had promised me that I should have permission—the mild and melancholy letter of a woman who dreaded the agitations of a meeting. After waiting for more than a month, I made bold to call, and desired Gobain to inquire whether I could be received. I sat down in a chair in the avenue near the lodge, my head buried in my hands, and there I remained for almost an hour.

""Madame had to dress," said Gobain, to hide Honorine's hesitancy under a pride of appearance which was flattering to me.

"'During a long quarter of an hour we both of us were possessed by an involuntary nervous trembling as great as that which seizes a speaker on the platform, and we spoke to each other sacred phrases, like those of persons taken by surprise who "make believe" a conversation.

""You see, Honorine," said I, my eyes full of tears, "the ice is broken, and I am so tremulous with happiness that you must forgive the incoherency of my language. It will be so for a long time yet."

""There is no crime in being in love with your wife," said she with a forced smile.

""Do me the favor," said I, "no longer to work as you do. I have heard from Madame Gobain that for three weeks you have been living on your savings; you have sixty thousand francs a year of your own, and if you cannot give me back your heart, at least do not abandon your fortune to me."

""I have long known your kindness," said she.

""Though you should prefer to remain here," said I, "and to preserve your independence; though the most ardent love should find no favor in your eyes, still, do not toil."

"'I gave her three certificates for twelve thousand francs a year each; she took them, opened them languidly, and after reading them through she gave me only a look as my reward. She fully understood that I was not offering her money, but freedom.

""I am conquered," said she, holding out her hand, which I kissed. "Come and see me as often as you like."

"'So she had done herself a violence in receiving me. Next day I found her armed with affected high spirits, and it took two months of habit before I saw her in her true character. But then it was like a delicious May, a springtime of love that gave me ineffable bliss; she was no longer afraid; she was studying me. Alas! when I proposed that she should go to England to return ostensibly to me, to our home, that she should resume her rank and live in our new residence, she was seized with alarm.

""Why not live always as we are?" she said.

"'I submitted without saying a word.

""'Is she making an experiment?" I asked myself as I left her. On my way from my own house to the Rue Saint-Maur thoughts of love had swelled in my heart, and I had said to myself, like a young man, "This evening she will yield."

"'All my real or affected force was blown to the winds by a smile, by a command from those proud, calm eyes, untouched by passion. I remembered the terrible words you once quoted to me, "Lucretia's dagger wrote in letters of blood the watchword of woman's charter—Liberty!" and they froze me. I felt imperatively how necessary to me was Honorine's consent, and how impossible it was to wring it from her. Could she guess the storms that distracted me when I left as when I came?

"'At last I painted my situation in a letter to her, giving up the attempt to speak of it. Honorine made no answer, and she was so sad that I made as though I had not written. I was deeply grieved by the idea that I could have distressed her; she read my heart and forgave me. And this was how. Three days ago she received me, for the first time, in her own blue-and-white room. It was bright with flowers, dressed, and lighted up. Honorine was in a dress that made her bewitching. Her hair framed that face that you know in its light curls; and in it were some sprays of Cape heath; she wore a white muslin gown, a white sash with long floating ends. You know what she is in such simplicity, but that day she was a bride, the Honorine of long past days. My joy was chilled at once, for her face was terribly grave; there were fires beneath the ice.

""'Octave," she said, "I will return as your wife when you will. But understand clearly that this submission has its dangers. I can be resigned ____"

"'I made a movement.

""'Yes," she went on, "I understand: resignation offends you, and you want what I cannot give—Love. Religion and pity led me to renounce my vow of solitude; you are here!" She paused.

""'At first," she went on, "you asked no more. Now you demand your wife. Well, here I give you Honorine, such as she is, without deceiving you as to what she will be.—What shall I be? A mother? I hope it. Believe me, I hope it eagerly. Try to change me; you have my consent; but if I should die, my dear, do not curse my memory, and do not set down to obstinacy what I should call the worship of the Ideal, if it were not more natural to call the indefinable feeling which must kill me the worship of the Divine! The future will be nothing to me; it will be your concern; consult your own mind."

"'And she sat down in the calm attitude you used to admire, and watched me turning pale with the pain she had inflicted. My blood ran cold. On seeing the effect of her words she took both my hands, and, holding them in her own, she said:

"""Octave, I do love you, but not in the way you wish to be loved. I love your soul.... Still, understand that I love you enough to die in your service like an Eastern slave, and without a regret. It will be my expiation."

"'She did more; she knelt before me on a cushion, and in a spirit of sublime charity she said:

"""And perhaps I shall not die!"

"'For two months now I have been struggling with myself. What shall I do? My heart is too full; I therefore seek a friend, and send out this cry, "What shall I do?"'

"I did not answer this letter. Two months later the newspapers announced the return on board an English vessel of the Comtesse Octave, restored to her family after adventures by land and sea, invented with sufficient probability to arouse no contradiction.

"When I moved to Genoa I received a formal announcement of the happy event of the birth of a son to the Count and Countess. I held that letter in my hand for two hours, sitting on this terrace—on this bench. Two months after, urged by Octave, by M. de Grandville, and Monsieur de Serizy, my kind friends, and broken by the death of my uncle, I agreed to take a wife.

"Six months after the revolution of July I received this letter, which concludes the story of this couple:—

"'MONSIEUR MAURICE,—I am dying though I am a mother—perhaps because I am a mother. I have played my part as a wife well; I have deceived my husband. I have had happiness not less genuine than the tears shed by actresses on the stage. I am dying for society, for the family, for marriage, as the early Christians died for God! I know not of what I am dying, and I am honestly trying to find out, for I am not perverse; but I am bent on explaining my malady to you—you who brought that heavenly physician your uncle, at whose word I surrendered. He was my director; I nursed him in his last illness, and he showed me the way to heaven, bidding me persevere in my duty.

"'And I have done my duty.

"'I do not blame those who forget. I admire them as strong and necessary natures; but I have the malady of memory! I have not been able twice to feel that love of the heart which identifies a woman with the man she loves. To the last moment, as you know, I cried to your heart, in the confessional, and to my husband, "Have mercy!" But there was no mercy. Well, and I am dying, dying with stupendous courage. No courtesan was ever more gay than I. My poor Octave is happy; I let his love feed on the illusions of my heart. I throw all my powers into this terrible masquerade; the actress is applauded, feasted, smothered in flowers; but the invisible rival comes every day to seek its prey —a fragment of my life. I am rent and I smile. I smile on two children, but it is the elder, the dead one, that will triumph! I told you so before. The dead child calls me, and I am going to him.

"'The intimacy of marriage without love is a position in which my soul feels degraded every hour. I can never weep or give myself up to dreams but when I am alone. The exigencies of society, the care of my child, and that of Octave's happiness never leave me a moment to refresh myself, to renew my strength, as I could in my solitude. The incessant need for watchfulness startles my heart with constant alarms. I have not succeeded in implanting in my soul the sharp-eared vigilance that lies with facility, and has the eyes of a lynx. It is not the lip of one I love that drinks my tears and kisses them; my burning eyes are cooled with water, and not with tender lips. It is my soul that acts a part, and that perhaps is why I am dying! I lock up my griefs with so much care that nothing is to be seen of it; it must eat into something, and it has attacked my life.

"'I said to the doctors, who discovered my secret, "Make me die of some plausible complaint, or I shall drag my husband with me."

"'So it is quite understood by M. Desplein, Bianchon, and myself that I am dying of the softening of some bone which science has fully described. Octave believes that I adore him, do you understand? So I am afraid lest he should follow me. I now write to beg you in that case to be the little Count's guardian. You will find with this a codicil in which I have expressed my wish; but do not produce it excepting in case of need, for perhaps I am fatuously vain. My devotion may perhaps leave Octave inconsolable but willing to live. —Poor Octave! I wish him a better wife than I am, for he deserves to be well loved.

"'Since my spiritual spy is married, I bid him remember what the florist of the Rue Saint-Maur hereby bequeaths to him as a lesson: May your wife soon be a mother! Fling her into the vulgarest materialism of household life; hinder her from cherishing in her heart the mysterious flower of the Ideal—of that heavenly perfection in which I believed, that enchanted blossom with glorious colors, and whose perfume disgusts us with reality. I am a Saint-Theresa who has not been suffered to live on ecstasy in the depths of a convent, with the

Holy Infant, and a spotless winged angel to come and go as she wished.

"'You saw me happy among my beloved flowers. I did not tell you all: I saw love budding under your affected madness, and I concealed from you my thoughts, my poetry; I did not admit you to my kingdom of beauty. Well, well; you will love my child for love of me if he should one day lose his poor father. Keep my secrets as the grave will keep them. Do not mourn for me; I have been dead this many a day, if Saint Bernard was right in saying that where there is no more love there is no more life.'"

"And the Countess died," said the Consul, putting away the letters and locking the pocket-book.

"Is the Count still living?" asked the Ambassador, "for since the revolution of July he has disappeared from the political stage."

"Do you remember, Monsieur de Lora," said the Consul-General, "having seen me going to the steamboat with——"

"A white-haired man! an old man?" said the painter.

"An old man of forty-five, going in search of health and amusement in Southern Italy. That old man was my poor friend, my patron, passing through Genoa to take leave of me and place his will in my hands. He appoints me his son's guardian. I had no occasion to tell him of Honorine's wishes."

"Does he suspect himself of murder?" said Mademoiselle des Touches to the Baron de l'Hostal.

"He suspects the truth," replied the Consul, "and that is what is killing him. I remained on board the steam packet that was to take him to Naples till it was out of the roadstead; a small boat brought me back. We sat for some little time taking leave of each other—for ever, I fear. God only knows how much we love the confidant of our love when she who inspired it is no more.

"'That man,' said Octave, 'holds a charm and wears an aureole.' the Count went to the prow and looked down on the Mediterranean. It happened to be fine, and, moved no doubt by the spectacle, he spoke these last words: 'Ought we not, in the interests of human nature, to inquire what is the irresistible power which leads us to sacrifice an exquisite creature to the most fugitive of all pleasures, and in spite of our reason? In my conscience I heard cries. Honorine was not alone in her anguish. And yet I would have it!... I am consumed by remorse. In the Rue Payenne I was dying of the joys I had not; now I shall die in Italy of the joys I have had.... Wherein lay the discord between two natures, equally noble, I dare assert?'"

For some minutes profound silence reigned on the terrace.

Then the Consul, turning to the two women, asked, "Was she virtuous?"

Mademoiselle des Touches rose, took the Consul's arm, went a few steps away, and said to him:

"Are not men wrong too when they come to us and make a young girl a wife while cherishing at the bottom of their heart some angelic image, and comparing us to those unknown rivals, to perfections often borrowed from a remembrance, and always finding us wanting?"

"Mademoiselle, you would be right if marriage were based on passion; and that was the mistake of those two, who will soon be no more. Marriage with heart-deep love on both sides would be Paradise."

Mademoiselle des Touches turned from the Consul, and was immediately joined by Claude Vignon, who said in her ear:

"A bit of a coxcomb is M. de l'Hostal."

"No," replied she, whispering to Claude these words: "for he has not yet guessed that Honorine would have loved him.—Oh!" she exclaimed, seeing the Consul's wife approaching, "his wife was listening! Unhappy man!"

Eleven was striking by all the clocks, and the guests went home on foot along the seashore.

"Still, that is not life," said Mademoiselle des Touches. "That woman was one of the rarest, and perhaps the most extraordinary exceptions in intellect—a pearl! Life is made up of various incidents, of pain and pleasure alternately. The Paradise of Dante, that sublime expression of the ideal, that perpetual blue, is to be found only in the soul; to ask it of the facts of life is a luxury against which nature protests every hour. To such souls as those the six feet of a cell, and the kneeling chair are all they need."

"You are right," said Leon de Lora; "but good-for-nothing as I may be, I cannot help admiring a woman who is capable, as that one was, of living by the side of a studio, under a painter's roof, and never coming down, nor seeing the world, nor dipping her feet in the street mud."

"Such a thing has been known—for a few months," said Claude Vignon, with deep irony.

"Comtesse Honorine is not unique of her kind," replied the Ambassador to Mademoiselle des Touches. "A man, nay, and a politician, a bitter writer, was the object of such a passion; and the pistol shot which killed him hit not him alone; the woman who loved lived like a nun ever after."

"Then there are yet some great souls in this age!" said Camille Maupin, and she stood for some minutes pensively leaning on the balustrade of the quay.

ADDENDUM

The following personages appear in other stories of the Human Comedy.

Bauvan, Comte Octave de
    Scenes from a Courtesan's Life

  Bianchon, Horace
    Father Goriot
    The Atheist's Mass
    Cesar Birotteau
    The Commission in Lunacy
    Lost Illusions
    A Distinguished Provincial at Paris
    A Bachelor's Establishment
    The Secrets of a Princess
    The Government Clerks
    Pierrette
    A Study of Woman
    Scenes from a Courtesan's Life
    The Seamy Side of History
    The Magic Skin
    A Second Home
    A Prince of Bohemia
    Letters of Two Brides
    The Muse of the Department
    The Imaginary Mistress
    The Middle Classes
    Cousin Betty
    The Country Parson
In addition, M. Bianchon narrated the following:
    Another Study of Woman
    La Grande Breteche

  Desplein
    The Atheist's Mass
    Cousin Pons
    Lost Illusions
    The Thirteen
    The Government Clerks
    Pierrette
    A Bachelor's Establishment
    The Seamy Side of History
    Modeste Mignon
    Scenes from a Courtesan's Life

  Fontanon, Abbe
    A Second Home
    The Government Clerks
    The Member for Arcis

  Gaudissart, Felix
    Scenes from a Courtesan's Life
    Cousin Pons
    Cesar Birotteau
    Gaudissart the Great

  Gaudron, Abbe
    The Government Clerks
    A Start in Life

Granville, Vicomte de (later Comte)
  The Gondreville Mystery
  A Second Home
  Farewell (Adieu)
  Cesar Birotteau
  Scenes from a Courtesan's Life
  A Daughter of Eve
  Cousin Pons

Lora, Leon de
  The Unconscious Humorists
  A Bachelor's Establishment
  A Start in Life
  Pierre Grassou
  Cousin Betty
  Beatrix

Loraux, Abbe
  A Start in Life
  A Bachelor's Establishment
  Cesar Birotteau

Popinot, Jean-Jules
  Cesar Birotteau
  The Commission in Lunacy
  The Seamy Side of History
  The Middle Classes

Serizy, Comte Hugret de
  A Start in Life
  A Bachelor's Establishment
  Modeste Mignon
  Scenes from a Courtesan's Life

Touches, Mademoiselle Felicite des
  Beatrix
  Lost Illusions
  A Distinguished Provincial at Paris
  A Bachelor's Establishment
  Another Study of Woman
  A Daughter of Eve
  Beatrix
  The Muse of the Department

Vignon, Claude
  A Distinguished Provincial at Paris
  A Daughter of Eve
  Honorine
  Beatrix
  Cousin Betty
  The Unconscious Humorists

Lightning Source UK Ltd.
Milton Keynes UK
UKHW040922021019
350834UK00003B/270/P